SHADOW LINE

SHADOW LINE

WAS MICK AN UNDERCOVER COP PRETENDING
TO BE A CRIMINAL OR A CRIMINAL
PRETENDING NOT TO BE? IN THE SHADOWS IT
WAS HARD TO TELL

V. J. HARRIS

SHADOW LINE

Independently published

Copyright © 2026 V. J. Harris

All rights reserved

ISBN-13: 979-8278818632

❀ Formatted with Vellum

This work of fiction is for all those undercover officers who walked in the shadows, often unseen, often unheard, rarely fully understood, and whose true stories may never be told.

INTRODUCTION

Brummie, Mick Dorrington, was once a successful undercover police officer. Whenever the job demanded someone to step into the shadows, Mick was the one who volunteered. No matter how dangerous, how dirty, or how much it would cost him. That, more than his talent, was why they kept calling his name. But a lifetime lived in the shadows leaves scars, and when a long-term infiltration into a Liverpool drugs gang is abruptly shut down, Mick learns just how steep the personal cost can be.

Cast aside by the service he devoted his life to, manipulated by senior officers he trusted, and betrayed by the woman he should never have loved, Mick is left to rebuild a life that no longer feels like his own.

Flawed, bruised, but still governed by a stubborn sense of right and wrong, he reinvents himself on society's margins—part investigator, part protector, part ghost—haunted by the lines he crossed and the man he might have become.

Years later, Mick is dragged back into the darkness when Aiden, a young man trapped in a Liverpool sex-trafficking ring, crosses his path. Protecting him forces Mick to confront violent criminals, buried truths, and the one name from his past he hoped never to face again. And beneath it all lies the secret the police once buried to protect themselves.

Introduction

Shadow Lineis a gritty, intimate noir thriller about the psychological toll of deep-cover work, the corrosive weight of institutional betrayal, and one man's fragile attempt to do right—even when the shadows have already claimed too much of him.

1

THE LONG SHADOW

Wherever he went Mick Dorrington drew eyes. People nodded, stepped aside, shifted their weight—whether they knew him or not. Most didn't, and most preferred it that way, but Mick had a presence that travelled ahead of him like a long shadow. Not loud; not threatening. Just... inevitable. He carried the look of a man who'd walked through places and who'd seen things others only had nightmares about, and who'd done things no one would admit to imagining. World-worn; street-sharp. A solitary figure, though not entirely unapproachable, if the need was dire enough.

What most people thought they knew about him was mostly wrong. They guessed late fifties, maybe early sixties. Someone once muttered, "He's done a stretch, you can tell—got that prison pallor," which Mick had found quietly amusing. Let them think what they liked, rumours hung off him like cigarette smoke—ex-Forces, hitman, bodyguard, spook he'd heard them all. Wild stories whispered by people who wanted to sound like they'd seen something of the world. People who wanted to believe that they knew him, or who wanted other people to believe that they knew him. Friends and acquaintances that he never knew he had. He always made the most of it.

No one ever came close to the truth; Mick made sure of that. His past stayed locked behind eyes that had learned never to give anything away. Most didn't ask questions of him, those who did got rehearsed responses that satisfied their curiosity but betrayed nothing.

He sat in his favourite chair in the snug at The Brikkies, the cracked leather molded to his backside like it had been waiting for him all day. A brandy sweated quietly on the table in front of him, untouched for the best part of twenty minutes, while he stared through it and let his thoughts wander where they pleased.

"Cheer up, bab – might never happen."

The voice, still with a hint of the Black Country evident, lit the air beside him like a match. Mick blinked, dragged himself back from wherever he'd been and found Trina standing there, hands on hips, eyes full of mischief and concern in equal measure.

"I'm all right, Trina," he said, voice low, steady, "Just thinkin'; reminiscing, that's all."

Trina, early forties, vivacious, attractive, called herself a masseuse on good days, a dancer on others. Both descriptions fitted but neither covered half of it. Hers was a story the city had heard too many times. Her mom, Kayleigh, Wolverhampton born, got pregnant at fifteen while in care. Social tried their best to keep them together but before Trina turned one, Kayleigh had shacked up with a bloke who was too handy with his fists. The bruises didn't go unnoticed. Trina was taken back into the system and stayed there fifteen long and mostly unhappy years. She never heard from Kayleigh again. Word was the woman had run errands for a drug crew, lost a shipment of 'Charlie' and vanished the way people do when debts outweigh their usefulness.

Now some kids make it out of the care system and find stability. Trina wasn't one of them. Hers was a story of frequent moves and instability. A cycle of being moved between various placements, foster homes, residential care homes and occasional abuse, which only led to feelings of loneliness and despair. The emotional toll led to depression and self-harm. She mostly felt worthless - at least until she reached her teens. Those who cared for her quietly began to worry as she blossomed into a very pretty young woman far too early. A pretty young woman who lacked life skills and emotional literacy. She had been "kept" rather than cared for. She lacked the kind of nurturing that might have given her the tools to navigate through life. But Trina wasn't blind. She began to notice the glances she got from strangers, particularly from men. Little more than a child, but already she knew that not everything was stacked against her.

Barely fifteen, Trina packed what little she had of any value into a small case and walked out the care home door like she was late for an important appointment. Wearing her best miniskirt and leather jacket she hitched a ride to 'Brum', the second largest city in the country.

Brum was the short nickname for the City of Birmingham, which was a name derived from the older local label of 'Brummagem', as the area had been known since the Middle Ages. Over time, Brummagem, a place of industry and endeavour became associated with counterfeit goods, but the shortened version, 'Brum', persisted and became a widely used proud nickname for the city. Its inhabitants were widely and popularly known as 'Brummies'.

Slim but curvaceous, a shock of red hair, sharp green eyes and with makeup she looked older than her years. She was picked up in under seven minutes. A couple more and she'd talked the driver into detouring to Moseley Village.

"Cool spot, so I've been told," she'd said to the driver, but nowhere near where he'd been planning on going.

She'd also sold him on, "Fifty quid gets you the best blow job You've ever had."

First time either of them had done anything like it, but she walked away knowing one thing for certain: she'd never be skint again. She figured that there were too many lonely men with too much money and too little willpower. She could get anything she wanted, if she could convince them that they could too. What she didn't know—what she couldn't—was how many men were out there watching for girls like her. Men who treated a young runaway like a winning lottery ticket. That was why Mick was destined to enter her life.

- - - - -

It was an early December evening in 2003, when Mick decided to take a bottle of Bells Whisky to an old contact, Jacob, who lived in a wharf-side penthouse in the middle of Brum.

Jacob was still technically in business with his estranged wife, Harriet, the real brains behind their "executive massage" empire. Half a dozen parlours scattered across the city, all gleaming on the surface, all run with Harriet's steel discipline. She insisted Jacob kept well away from the premises and especially away from the girls. She'd always suspected he got a little too friendly for her liking. Truth was, Jacob cared about those girls more than he ever said, but he loved Harriet too much to stray. Even after they split, he'd taken the fall when Vice ran a covert operation and taped several girls offering 'extras' to undercover cops. Jacob offered to take the fall, on one condition: Harriet walked.

The police didn't argue. It was a quick win. Jacob pleaded guilty to six counts of living off immoral earnings and served six months of an eighteen-month stretch. At that time Mick had known him a couple of years through mutual contacts and had even used the services of his parlours once or twice, not something either of them discussed.

Before going inside to do his time, Jacob had asked Mick to keep an eye on Harriet. Mick didn't hesitate and more than once he had stepped in to warn off competitors who had an eye on the business while Jacob was otherwise engaged, although his friend wasn't exactly new to the prison system. The old borstal-spot tattoo on his cheek gave away more than Jacob ever said - troubled teenage years from before they rebranded those places as Youth Custody Centres.

The borstals had been all discipline, hard graft and compulsory lessons, which failed to straighten Jacob out, not fully, but they did knock the violence out of him. He decided there were easier ways to survive than throwing punches. Plenty of working girls needed someone to keep an eye on them, a father figure of sorts, to make sure they stayed safe, stayed healthy, stayed earning.

Jacob stepped into that role with a gentleness that surprised most people. Unusual as it sounded, the girls he looked after genuinely cared for him. And then he met Harriet, a working girl with a vision and the discipline to achieve her aims. They clicked immediately. He had never looked back until their marriage ran out of steam.

They were still a decent business team. Truth is, they needed each other more than Harriet dared to admit.

Mick parked his BMW Z3 Roadster on Livery Street and walked the short distance to 'The Old Contemptibles", or locally known as simply, 'The OCs", a Victorian corner pub with high ceilings and an oak-panelled bar.

Mick didn't use the place often. Too many off-duty cops drifted in from a local police station and Police HQ, both just a stone's throw away, and he'd never liked being anywhere near that sort of company. But tonight was late enough that the daytime peelers would be long gone and too early for the late shift guys. Just civilians left, the regulars and the curious.

The OC's had good ale on tap, but Mick ordered a brandy. The barman asked his preference; Mick didn't have one. He was poured a Hennessy without ceremony.

Eyes followed him as he crossed the room, most people clocked him when he walked in anywhere. A pair of well-heeled corporate secretary types in their forties glanced over, muttered something to each other, and giggled behind their glasses like schoolgirls.

Four men in matching blue pinstripes, obviously briefs from a local Chambers by the look of them, were holding court at a corner table, laughing too loudly, the kind of laugh that only comes after a day spent billing clients for bad news. Heavy leather briefcases sat by their feet like obedient dogs.

Two old boys, fixtures of the place, were giving far too much attention to a group of girls in their early twenties who'd picked the OC's as a meet-up spot before heading for the brighter lights.

Birthday drinks, by the sound of it. Too much perfume, too much flesh, too much laughter, the kind that comes before mistakes.

Mick took his brandy and moved away from the bar, letting the heat of the place brush against him without ever breaking the chill he carried inside.

By the time he'd sat down, he'd already taken the whole room apart in his head. Details came to him the way breath came to others, automatic, uninvited, necessary. What had once been survival had settled into habit.

The barman who poured his drink was right-handed, but the nails on his left hand were clipped down to nothing. Guitarist, Mick guessed—short nails for the fretting hand.

One of the pinstriped briefs had a dusting of white powder on his tie and a persistent little sniff that might have been hay fever, if it weren't December.

One of the giggling secretaries had a pale band on her ring finger —recently shed her wedding ring, recently shed a husband. Explained the laughter that didn't quite reach her eyes.

And one of the birthday girls was nursing tonic water, watching her friends get louder and looser while she stayed perfectly still. She wasn't having fun. Mick figured she'd already made her mistake.

He had trained himself out of the old habit—glancing at the door every time it opened. A man who did that marked himself as someone with something to hide, or someone expecting trouble. Mick was neither, not anymore. But he still watched the ones who did look up. They always told him something.

So, he kept his eyes on his drink when the slim redhead stumbled into The Old Contemptibles, her arm clamped tight in the grip of the man steering her. As they passed, Mick caught the sharp hit of Tommy Girl , too recently, and too heavily sprayed, and beneath it, the sour mix of cigarettes and stale beer rolling off the escort.

One glance told him they weren't a couple. He was a little too old to be a boyfriend, too young to be her dad. Too controlling for either. For the briefest moment, the girl's eyes met his. Panic, resignation, and a message as clear as spoken words: "I'm in trouble. You can't help me. Don't get involved."

Mick answered her with the faintest smile, calm, steady, unthreatening. It landed. Something in the way she exhaled told him she felt safer just knowing he was in the room. Someone who wouldn't judge the situation she had been forced into. Someone who might actually see her.

Her escort snapped his fingers. She emptied her small leather purse into his palm without hesitation. Mick judged the bundle, maybe a ton's worth. He knew exactly how she'd earned it, and exactly what she was.

The man then dumped her at a table near Mick's and told her to 'sit and stay' like she was a dog. Then he strode to the bar, glancing back every few steps to make sure she hadn't dared to move.

Trina hadn't been in Brum long. A few months, maybe. She'd drifted into Moseley thinking it was a village , it wasn't. Just a suburb with a bohemian heart, three miles from the city centre and a world away in attitude.

Squats everywhere. Students, musos, artists, hippies, daydreamers. The kind of place where you could wander into a pub and bump into some of Brum's success stories, bands who had tasted considerable success, but who were still just Brummies at heart, or one of the local eccentrics like 'Tall Paul' Fitzgerald, a self-proclaimed hippy who'd walked everywhere on stilts for decades, because he claimed it was healthier than being too close to the pavement. Everyone knew 'Tall Paul'. Everyone knew everyone.

With the Balti Triangle, an area on the borders of Moseley and neighbouring Sparkhill, where Indian chefs had opened up restaurants that specialised in cheap but tasty dishes cooked in a 'Balti', a sort of Indian wok, just a short walk away, and enough bars and restaurants to suit any mood, Moseley had a vibe that hooked her quick. It was exactly the "cool spot" she'd hoped for. She made friends fast, the kind of friends who'd make sure she never slept out in the cold.

It didn't take long for Ronnie Dale to find her. Early-thirties, flash motor, expensive threads, taste for anything showy. Called himself a 'Talent Spotter.' Her new mates warned her off, said they'd heard "bad shit" about him, but Ronnie offered the sort of life she'd only ever imagined. Or at least he pretended to. Truth was, Ronnie worked for his old man, Paul Dale, who ran escort agencies and so called Kissogram outfits that were nothing of the sort, just pipelines feeding young girls to high-paying clients with filthy appetites.

Ronnie knew about Trina within a day of her landing in Moseley. Kept tabs on her until he had the time to stage the perfect "accidental" meeting. To him, she was just another winning lottery ticket waiting to be cashed.

Trina enjoyed the shine for a while; the restaurants with starched tablecloths, the clubs where the lights caught her hair just right, the way Ronnie paraded her like she was something rare. And she let herself enjoy it. Why shouldn't she? But she wasn't stupid. She was waiting for the punchline. Girls like her always knew one was coming. She didn't have to wait long. Just didn't see it fast enough.

Ronnie spun her a story about some "dodgy geezer" blackmailing him with a cooked-up rape allegation. He swore blind he'd been set up, couldn't prove a thing, needed to retaliate before his life fell apart. The plan sounded simple enough: Trina would move into a flat he'd sorted, hers afterward, rent-free, and she'd lure this geezer round under the pretence of meeting Ronnie. Once he arrived, she'd charm him, entertain him, "treat him nicely... give him head, fuck him if you want, he'll pay," Ronnie said, as if he were discussing the weather. Then he'd get the footage he needed to shut the man up.

The alarms were faint, but they were there. Still, she told herself it was one favour, one performance. Do this, keep Ronnie sweet, then look for a way out. It didn't go that way. Ronnie had fed the same tale to so many girls he'd stopped keeping count. Trina was just the latest one plucked off the street and polished up. He drove her to a smart flat near Gas Street Basin—a clean, modern place, too nice for someone like her, which made it feel dangerous. He dropped the keys in her hand and said the blackmailer would be there within the hour. That was it. No warmth. No goodbye.

She played the part perfectly when the knock came. She offered the visitor a drink, made small talk about waiting for Ronnie to get home. She smiled when she needed to smile. Flirted just enough.

Led him toward the bedroom when he responded the way all men in his position responded. He was repulsive, but she had survived worse. She told herself to think of the flat. Think of a future. Think of anything but him.

"You're gorgeous," he said, leering as he loosened his tie. "What do I call you?"

"Trina," she said lightly. "And you?"

"You can call me Mr Dale. I believe you know my lad Ronnie. I must say..." He looked her up and down with a slow, filthy grin. "He's excelled himself this time."

The meaning hit her in pieces. First the name. Then the grin. Then the truth, dropping into her gut like a stone. Paul Dale. Not the blackmailer. The architect. She didn't scream. Didn't fight. She knew better. Every instinct told her resistance would be pointless, dangerous, and loud - loud enough to ruin her, not enough to save her. So, she shut her eyes and let her mind crawl anywhere else but the bed beneath her.

When it was over, he wiped himself on the sheets without looking at her, got dressed as though fixing a minor inconvenience, and finally turned her way with a scowl.

"You work for me now. You'd better wise up fast. My clients have... very specific tastes. I Don't want complaints. Ronnie'll be back in a minute to give you the rules."

He fished a wad of notes from his pocket and tossed them onto the floor like rubbish.

"Make sure Ronnie gets that. You'll get your share". A brief stifled snorting laugh. "Hope you like the flat." Then he walked out.

Trina didn't cry. Crying required hope that someone might hear you, or care if they did. In that silent flat, she had no such illusions.

She hadn't met Mick yet.

Trina had toyed with the idea of throwing on a few clothes and vanishing into the night, but barely two minutes had passed before she heard Ronnie's key scrape the lock.

"Get dressed," he barked. "I need a drink—and you need to know the score."

In the years that followed, that night never drifted far from her thoughts. She could never figure out why Ronnie had hauled her to that particular bar, or why the weathered man with the tattoos and the tired-but handsome face struck her, instantly, as someone she could trust. And why he had looked at her in a way that seemed to fleetingly suggest that they had met before. They hadn't. Some things you don't reason your way through. Some things just are.

Ronnie slouched back to their table carrying a pint for himself and a Bacardi Breezer for her. From across the room Mick watched the scene unfold, silent and still, giving nothing away. He didn't need to hear the words; the body language told the whole sorry story. Ronnie, all whispered menace and cheap swagger, leaning in on a girl who had already run out of options.

Mick had met the real monsters—the brutes, the psychos, the men who didn't need to advertise their cruelty. Ronnie wasn't one of them. He was a small-time bully in a big coat, riding the reputation of a father much darker than he was. He walked like he owned the city. He didn't.

The silent movie reached its finale. Mick drained the last of his brandy, placed the empty glass on the bar, and left before the barman could ask if he wanted another. Outside, a dusting of snow softened the street, though it wouldn't survive the night. Mick flipped his collar up against the cold and slipped into the dark.

Trina remembered only flashes of what happened next. She followed Ronnie out the same door Mick had taken moments earlier, trailing two paces behind as Ronnie swaggered along Edmund Street and cut right into Livery Street.

She didn't see Mick emerge from the shadows. She only saw Ronnie fold, hard, after a fist like a sledgehammer buried itself in his ribs. The breath shot out of him in a sick, wet grunt, half air and half ale. Before Ronnie could recover, Mick draped an arm around his shoulders as if greeting an old friend. He leaned in close, voice low but gentle.

"Do me a favour and tell your father that Micky Dee sends his compliments. Let him know I understand the whole thing was a mix-up, no way he knew Trina here was... spoken for. No hard feelings."

Then he turned to her. "Trina, love, do you have anything that isn't yours?"

She said nothing, just handed over the flat keys Ronnie had given her earlier and which Mick placed neatly into Ronnie's shaking hand.

"You'll be wantin' these back. Right then. Lovely meeting you. Remember, best wishes to your old man. C'mon, Trina."

For a heartbeat she froze. Who the hell was this Micky Dee? How did he know her name? Ronnie's father's name? Why was he helping her? Was this rescue—or recruitment? Was she safer with him, or safer running?

Mick took her hand, careful and slow. He looked her in the eyes.

"You've got a thousand questions. You'll get your answers in time. You can walk away now if that's what you want. Or I can walk you to the station and give you the fare to anywhere you choose, no questions asked. And if you're wondering why... well, that's a longer tale. For now, you need somewhere safe. Someone decent to look out for you."

"And that's you?" she asked.

"Oh no," he said with a small, tired smile. "I work better alone. But I know someone. Someone who'll treat you right."

And for reasons she couldn't name, Trina believed him. Maybe it was hope, maybe desperation. Maybe fate. Either way, she made the right choice.

Later that evening, Jacob lifted a glass of freshly opened Bells and offered a quiet, wordless toast to his old mate Mick. Just a few feet away, Trina slept safely, soundly, for the first time in longer than she could remember. Girls like Trina don't get fairytales, not really. But this..., this was as close as the world was ever likely to give her.

2

THE RISE OF A FEARLESS MAN

The Observer newspaper ran a piece in May '95 about the surge of gang violence tearing through Liverpool, shootings of known "faces" becoming a daily headline. The city was in the middle of a street-level war for the drugs trade, and the crown went to whoever was ruthless enough to take it. During those turf wars, even the old hands slipped out of town when they could. Reputation didn't matter. Names didn't matter. Nobody was safe. A few wide-eyed chancers tried muscling their way into the chaos, more ego than sense. One or two lived long enough to brag about it. Most didn't. Some vanished into the night. Others didn't get the chance.

Around that time, the "Bizzies", as the locals in Liverpool uniquely referred to the police, started picking up whispers about a lowlife named Victor Harland, his name rising fast through the city's criminal food chain. While many of the real players were fleeing the city as the chaos peaked, Harland stepped neatly into the empty shoes they left behind. He thrived in the madness. Gangs stripped of leadership needed someone to point the way, and Harland was only too happy to oblige. Risky? Of course, but Victor Harland was a man who feared nothing. Literally nothing.

Victor was the only son of Anders Haaland, a former Norwegian merchant seaman, and Lily McAvoy, whose family had drifted up to Southport in the seventies to escape the poverty grinding Liverpool into the dirt. Their roots might have started in Scotland, but Liverpool had carved itself deep into them by the time she met Anders. Her man had come to the UK in '71, picking up a job shifting containers at the Liverpool docks thanks to old Merchant Navy contacts. He met Lily on a night out neither expected to turn into anything. They were aiming for a few hours of company, nothing more, but Cupid had other plans.

Two months later they were at the Liverpool Register Office, tying the knot, with a couple of buskers they'd pulled in from outside the Cavern Club serving as witnesses. Beatles melodies, loose change in a guitar case, and a tenner each for watching strangers get married—it was too good a gig to pass up. They even bought a box of confetti and threw it over the couple before heading back to their pitch.

Anders and Lily managed exactly fifteen weeks of married life. Then Anders volunteered for an extra shift at the docks—trying to put a little more aside for their house fund. Two days later, The Liverpool Echo ran a grim headline. Police and H.M Customs were investigating the death of a dockworker, crushed under a falling container while securing a stack. A "tragic accident," an HMC source had said. No one else harmed. No one else involved.

A distressed Lily found out from a young copper whose uniform still creaked like it had just come off the hanger. He couldn't have been more than fifteen in the face. She made him a cup of tea, thanked him for the sympathy he barely managed to express. She guessed—correctly, that it was the first death message he'd ever delivered. It wouldn't be his last.

Lily spent what little they'd scraped together to give Anders a proper send-off. She hadn't planned for the funeral to fall on the sixmonth anniversary of the night they met, fate just had a cruel sense of humour. Half a year; that was all she'd had with a good man, a gentle man, someone she knew would've been a loving husband and an even better father. They would have found a house, filled it with noise, kids, and a life worth living. Instead, she stood in a rented room with grief gnawing at her ribs when the thought hit her like a slap.

Shit. Filled the house with kids! She'd been so buried in funeral arrangements and phone calls and the dead weight of grief, and she hadn't noticed the thing she should have. She was late. Proper late. They'd been trying, in their shy, hopeful way, for a family. Anders had insisted they should have children while they were still young enough to enjoy them. His own father had been grey and tired by the time Anders arrived, and they'd never had much to say to each other. He didn't want that for his own kids.

Lily had always dreamed of being a mum. She'd never dreamed of doing it alone.

The 'Clearblue' test she'd rushed to buy confirmed what she already half knew. Pregnant. A million thoughts crashed through her mind at once.

Pragmatism stepped in first: I'll have to end it. I can't raise a child on my own. Then idealism, soft but stubborn: It's ours. Mine and Anders. The last piece of him in the world.

Optimism flickered like a cheap light bulb: I'll manage. I'll make it work. Maybe someone decent will love the baby too.

And then the darkest voice, cold and brutally practical: I can't afford this. Not like this. Maybe adoption... maybe that's the only way out.

For the rest of that night, Lily sat at the small kitchen table in the Victorian terrace in the Wavertree suburb, staring at the test on the Formica like it might change its mind if she watched long enough. Outside, the city moved on without her—buses whining past, drunks laughing too loudly, the neighbours' arguing about money... again. Life, indifferent as always.

By dawn, nothing felt clearer, but the panic had burned off, leaving something quieter behind. Resolve, maybe. Or exhaustion wearing its mask.

She folded the test into its box, slid it into the drawer beside the sink, and then addressed the empty room in a whisper, "Alright then. It's you and me."

There was no ceremony to it. No tears. Just a simple acceptance that whatever came next, she'd face it. Anders hadn't asked for much out of life, but he'd wanted this, wanted a family, something of his own after years at sea and a childhood spent in the shadow of a man too old to raise him. Lily could almost hear him: 'Go on, Lil, the kid'll be grand.'

The months crawled by. The bump grew. Money didn't. Lily took odd jobs, shifts in cafés, scrubbed floors in offices after hours, did whatever she could to stay afloat. The house fund they'd been saving vanished into rent, bills, groceries, prams, baby grows. Her grief dulled but never disappeared. And then, one cold morning in February, the child arrived, a boy who responded to a midwife's shake with a bellowing scream, furious at being dragged into a cold world from a place of warmth and comfort.

"Blimey, he's got a good set of lungs on him. I think he wants his mum. What are you gonna call him?"

"Victor."

She chose the name because Anders had liked it. Said it sounded Norwegian, it sounded strong, like someone who wouldn't take a kicking from life without giving one back. Lily clung to that hope.

For the first few years, Lily managed. Just about. Victor grew fast, too fast, and with a glare that seemed older than his bones. His red hair and pale blue eyes were striking. By the time he could walk, he was running; by the time he could talk, he was arguing. Not badly. Not nastily. Just... sharply, like he was born with hard edges. Some kids inherit their parents' hair, their smile, their laugh. Victor was an enigma. Bright, determined, focused, and with a temper, he seemed courageous, rugged, and fearless. Yes, certainly fearless. Trying to raise a kid who just knew no fear drove Lily to despair.

"Don't touch that, it'll burn you;" "Don't run across the road;"

"Don't touch that dog;" "Don't put that in your mouth."

Parents will know the value of teaching kids to fear danger. Nothing seemed to intimidate Victor. It made life difficult. She spent more time in A&E than she should have, and Social Services started to take an interest in her.

Lily's despair was genuine, and that was the first clue that she wasn't a bad parent, she wasn't abusing Victor. There was another explanation. Sadly, it would be years before that explanation would be found and Lily would never learn that Victor had damage to a very small part of his brain, the Amygdala. A small part of the brain that had a very big job to do. It is where emotions are processed. It can reduce the ability to feel or learn from fear, and it can impair some-one's ability to recognise emotions in others. Those two symptoms were evident in Victor, but Lily just questioned where she was going wrong.

Lily tried. God, she tried. But as Victor grew older, bigger, louder... something changed. In his early teens he stopped asking questions and started making decisions. Wrong ones. Dangerous ones. Choices that made Lily's stomach twist every time he walked out the door. Yes, loads of kids did some of the things he did. Nicking sweets from the local shop, getting hold of a can of booze and puking it up, smoking a spliff over the local park. All rights of passage that all parents worry about, but which rarely have any long-term implica-tions. With Victor though, it was different. By the time he was fifteen, he was spelling his name differently, as if he wanted to create his own character, and the whispers had started—quiet at first, and then louder. A lad from Wavertree who spent his time in Toxteth, got a temper like a lit fuse. A kid who didn't flinch. A kid who didn't run. A kid who was going to end up in charge of something one day; he boasted as much. That day didn't take long.

THERE WAS A STORY ABOUT VICTOR, never confirmed, always whispered, that he'd risen fast in Toxteth's underworld. Word was he became a trusted lieutenant to Kenny Warton, one of the area's busiest traffickers. At first it was small deliveries, then debt collection, then handling the stubborn ones who couldn't, or wouldn't pay. He skimmed a little protection money along the way. It didn't take long before Victor earned a reputation- cross him and you'd regret it. Kenny valued that ruthlessness. That was his mistake.

On Victor's eighteenth birthday, Kenny summoned him to his office at the back of an unused vehicle repair garage , a small room contained within a bigger unit. The plan was a surprise celebration: a big cake, a few warm cans, and a sports bag stuffed with fifties, twenty grand as a thank-you bonus. Five of Kenny's top men were waiting. Baz Burgess, weighed down with gold chains and knuckle-breaking rings, flashing those ridiculous gold teeth, was there to "keep things light."

Victor walked in at precisely three o'clock to a round of applause. He didn't even smile. He reached inside his jacket, pulled out a Smith & Wesson 4506, and put two rounds through Kenny's face. Baz barely had time to inhale before Victor put a bullet in his chest. The remaining four lieutenants tensed, ready to charge. Victor casually swept the gun in their direction.

"Now then," he said, almost conversationally, "I liked Kenny and I like Baz...he's a lovely chap." He wandered over to Baz, who was writhing on the stained carpet square, and placed a final round through his forehead.

"Correction....he was a lovely chap." He paused staring at all four with inquisitive eyes, "So ask yourself this: if Victor here can shoot two men he actually liked, do you think he'd hesitate with any of you? Spoiler, the answer is 'no'. Now... who's coming on this journey with me? You'll never look back. You'll have everything you've ever wanted in your life. I will look after you and I'll look after those you love. Who's in, and who's out?"

Devlin, the only one Victor had truly expected loyalty from, pledged instantly. He'd seen Victor's potential from the first time they'd met. The O'Dowd brothers, Tom and Tony, gave stiff nods.

Victor made a mental note: he'd need a bit of insurance on them. So they were immediately assigned to clean up the office and to get rid of Kenny and Baz's corpses so that they couldn't be found...ever. Devlin would supervise. That would ensure that they stayed onside.

That left Jamie Grant. A newer face in Kenny's upper ranks, but reliable. Victor knew Jamie's girlfriend was pregnant, and that she'd been pushing him to get out.

"Am I right in thinking you want out, Jamie?"

The colour drained from Jamie's face. He hadn't said anything. How could Victor know. Victor nodded toward the sports bag. "How much in there?"

"About twenty grand," Jamie croaked, "It..., it was supposed to be for you."

"It's yours now. Take it."

Jamie stepped toward Kenny's slumped body and lifted the bag with trembling hands. He braced for the shot but never heard one.

"Look after that lady of yours," Victor said softly. "We're good."

Jamie swallowed hard, "I won't say a word, obviously."

"Oh, but you will," Victor replied, slowly and deliberately, "Not today, not tomorrow. But soon. You're going to tell everyone exactly what happened in this room. Every detail. Who died. Who watched. Who walked out alive. You won't need to tell the Bizzies , word will reach them in due course. And if you ever need anything... money, help, a problem solved... you come to me. And tell your friends, the ones you trust, that I'm hiring. The rewards will be good for the right people. References required, of course."

Jamie left with twenty grand and shaking hands, wondering what the hell had just happened. What he didn't know at that time, was this:

It was the day the legend of Victor Harland was born, and he'd had a pivotal role in that. It wouldn't be the last time that Jamie would feature in Harland's story. Not by a long way.

Just as he intended, Victor Harland grew feared and respected in equal measure. Before long, everyone in Liverpool knew his name. Everyone had heard the story. Even some of his fiercest rivals saw which way the wind was blowing and folded themselves neatly into his operation. Others whispered about taking his rising empire for themselves, but Victor understood the value of information better than most. His intelligence network kept him a step, or several steps ahead.

Competitors would get a warning...if they were lucky. If not, they vanished from the scene entirely. One way or another, Victor persuaded a few to leave Liverpool while they still had legs to run on.

The police, frustrated and increasingly embarrassed, leaned on their informants for anything they could find about him. They knew he controlled most of the cocaine moving through the city. They knew his lieutenants, his foot soldiers, his habits, his haunts. They tapped every phone he touched, shadowed him day and night, and kept a thick photographic file on him, so many pictures it looked more like a modelling portfolio than evidence.

Meanwhile, Victor diversified. He opened a car hire business. Then a haulage company. Then a pawn shop. Soon after, he had teams running duty-free cigarettes across borders, and sometimes people who were desperate enough to pay for silent passage into the country.

Bit by bit, piece by piece, Victor Harland stopped being just a name whispered in the dark and became something much more permanent. Something the city couldn't ignore.

He bought a big detached house out in West Kirby and talked his mum into moving there. She didn't need telling what he'd become, she'd seen the shadows gathering around him for years. Sometimes she wondered what Anders would have made of it all, his only son buying a house with blood-stained money scraped from the wrong side of the law. Living under that roof felt like a betrayal, both to her late husband and to the values she'd been raised with. But as they say in the 'Good Book'...needs must. And truth be told, she'd started to fear the gravity of the chaos that orbited Victor. If trouble was coming, and it always seemed to be near by, maybe distance was the only protection left to her. So, she packed her things, swallowed her guilt and let her boy move her somewhere quiet, somewhere safer... or at least safer than the place he came from.

Every so often the 'Bizzies' would storm one of his places, always tooled up; always loud about it. Firearms lads in the lead, dogs straining on their leashes: growlers, biters, sniffers, the full circus. And, just as Victor demanded, they were met with open doors and polite smiles. No attitude, no resistance, just cooperation so smooth it felt rehearsed.

There was a story, half rumour, half legend, that during a dawn raid on one of his units near Toxteth, the coppers walked into the smell of bacon sandwiches and fresh mugs of tea lined up on a counter. A CD player was blasting out Charles Penrose's, "The Laughing Policeman," each wheezing chuckle echoing around the warehouse like a private joke at the raiders' expense. The message couldn't have been clearer.

Harland lost count of the times he was arrested on suspicion of something or other, but he treated every collar like it was a minor inconvenience. Polite, respectful, silent. Always silent. He'd sit there in the interview room, immaculate suit, dead eyes revealing no emotions, no body language, and his solicitor parked beside him like a well-paid gargoyle.

He never answered a single question. Not one. He just smiled that slow, knowing curl of the lips that made detectives want to break chairs over his head, and his brief delivered the same rehearsed line: "Charge him, then. Let's all see this mountain of evidence you say you've got. My client is a legitimate and well-respected businessman. If some people are jealous of his success, that's hardly a crime."

And every time, Harland walked out the front door, smooth as silk.

Every now and then the police thought they finally had Harland boxed in. A dawn raid would hit the jackpot, kilos of coke stacked like bricks in a wall, enough to make any prosecutor salivate. But the trail never quite reached the man at the top. Instead, some bottom-of-the-ladder scally with a solicitor far too expensive for his pay grade would suddenly "cooperate," negotiate a tidy plea, and swallow the years that came his way without complaint. It didn't matter how long the stretch was. Their families would be looked after, envelopes would find their way through the right doors, and when they'd finally served their time, there'd be a big payday waiting. Harland had a roster of clean-record stooges ready to take the fall at a moment's notice. His insurance policies, bought and paid for.

By the age of 24, Victor Harland wasn't just confident; he was untouchable. He had friends in the police, favours stashed in the judiciary, and handshakes buried deep in local government guaranteeing no interruption in his affairs. He took care of them. They took care of him. And everyone else learned to keep out of his way. His rise had been remarkable. Liverpool was his - for now at least.

Detective Superintendent David 'Jock' McAllister was tasked with setting up a special operation into Harland. The directive came from the very top of the tree. He had been told that he could pick his own team people he could trust. There were no time constraints. Unusually, no limits on overtime or expenses, and whatever he needed he could have.

So far, all of the traditional policing methods had failed. Jock knew what he needed to do. He just had to find the right person to help him. But he wasn't even certain that such a person existed.

He hadn't met Mick yet.

3

GOING UNDER.

Mick Dorrington came into the world on a wet Tuesday in May 1964, in Marston Green Hospital, the sort of place where the ceilings were yellowed by steam and cigarette smoke, and the nurses all looked like they hadn't slept since the war.

His mother, Rita, never forgot the rain hammering the windows. Both Dennis and Rita Dorrington were Small Heath through and through, an inner city centre district which bred the kind of people described as 'salt of the earth' and they were no exception, until they were overheard to argue.

They'd met at the BSA factory back in '54, when Birmingham still made things and the skyline was a forest of chimneys. Dennis was already climbing the ladder, a production foreman, proud as brass, while Rita was a typist with fast fingers and a faster smile.

She said she liked him because he was confident. Later she admitted that she'd mistaken confidence for charm. He wasn't charming by any stretch of the imagination.

He had come from stock that had spent centuries breaking their backs in the Worcestershire and Gloucestershire farm fields, depending on which side of the shifting county line the government claimed they lived on that year.

His great-grandfather had walked all the way to Birmingham in search of work, following the trail of smoke and industry like a pilgrim heading for salvation. He found Small Heath instead, cramped terraces, clattering factories, and the kind of public houses where a man's reputation was worth more than his wage packet.

By the time Mick's grandfather arrived, the Dorrington's had become Birmingham people, and proud of it. No airs, no graces, no nonsense.

Dennis grew up tough. Not in the gangster sense, he had too much disdain for 'fancy lads with razors in their caps', but in the way of men who believed a fight behind the pub was as natural as a Sunday roast.

He boxed in the streets for shillings, earned a reputation as someone you didn't cross unless you fancied waking up in a gutter, and prided himself on working hard, drinking harder, and swinging punches hardest of all.

Even the local gangs knew of him, respected him and left him alone.

He went to church every Sunday, Bible under his arm, suit brushed, face shaved. He'd shake hands with the vicar like he was sealing a business deal. Claimed he was a Christian. Maybe he even believed it. But his Christianity came with Victorian values: women should know their place, children should speak when spoken to, and foreigners were "fine as long as they kept to their own." Rita endured it with the weary grace that women of her generation perfected.

Dennis believed a father's first duty was to teach his lad to box, and that served Mick well in the years that followed.

Rita, in contrast, was what Dennis liked to mockingly call 'airy-fairy'. She could paint, sew, darn, and, most remarkably, play the piano.

Family legend had it that her father brought home an old Packard upright to their house in Yardley, on the south side of Birmingham, planning to teach her a few tunes. The morning after it was delivered, the household woke to the sound of Over the Rainbow, played note-perfect by a girl who'd never had a lesson in her life. She'd adored the tune ever since her parents had taken her to the Kingston Cinema to see The Wizard of Oz. Over the next few days, her father summoned friends and neighbours to their humble home to witness what he called her 'God-given gift, there's no other explanation'. It was true; Rita could hear a tune once and play it perfectly.

People later compared her to Mrs Mills, the piano queen of the "60s and '70s.

"You could've done that if you'd got a bit more about you," Dennis would later sneer, perhaps regretting the meal ticket he felt she'd failed to become.

Rita loved reading, books, plays, poetry, anything that lifted her out of her life, even for an hour. She read constantly to Mick, even before he was a toddler.

They ploughed through the Janet and John and Ladybird series before he turned three. He was reading on his own before he was four, no encouragement needed. Books opened doors. Worlds. They allowed him to become someone else.

He devoured them through primary school and into secondary, choosing volumes that would bewilder most adults, Burroughs, Wallace, Huxley, Joyce, Hemingway, Shakespeare.

His teachers called him 'a conundrum'. He could dissect the trickiest texts with clarity that left them stunned, yet he refused to develop his academic potential.

Exams he passed, but rarely by more than the bare minimum, except English literature, where he excelled without trying. Talk of university was dismissed with a shrug. Mick already knew where his future lay. He'd known since he was eight.

IT WASN'T long after his eighth birthday that he had woken up to the sound of his father berating his mother over something trivial — probably a task he could've done himself. Dennis wasn't lazy, but inside the house he played the "master and breadwinner," and Rita served him like a maid.

Their relationship felt, to Mick, like something out of a period drama, and not the romantic kind. Sometimes he despised the man, his attitude to women, to migrants, to the unemployed, to anyone who wasn't a redblooded Brit willing to die for Queen and Country. Anyone who didn't agree with his prejudiced worldview.

Mick had once said that he loved drama and wanted to act on stage one day. Dennis had guffawed.

"Don't be soft, lad. We're having no bloody puffs in this house. You'll get a proper job."

That 'proper job' would be decided that very morning.

Mick dressed quietly and slipped out of the house while his parents traded insults with each other, the usual routine of bellowing, a slap, then tears. He didn't get far before realising he was running away from home. For good.

Like most eight-year-olds, he hadn't thought it through. He wandered through vaguely familiar backstreets, reached the Coventry Road, and turned right toward town, past St Andrew's Football Ground, head down and determined.

It seemed he'd walked for hours, whereby in truth, he'd dawdled for forty minutes before spotting the white-brick bulk of Digbeth police station. He sat on the steps, chewing on a stolen "finger of fudge," wondering if he should hand himself in as a missing person, or worse, a thief. His father always said, 'If you can't do the time, don't do the crime.'

"Hello, son. What you doing here then?" The voice boomed from apair of shiny boots that had been planted beside him.

Mick's eyes travelled up the blue serge uniform to a mustached face with rosy cheeks and deep brown eyes. The copper looked eight feet tall with his helmet on.

"I'm in trouble, and Mum said if I'm ever in trouble I should go to the police."

The giant crouched and sat beside him, removing the helmet. Not a giant. Just a man, a big one, but with a gentle smile.

"So what sort of trouble are you in, son?"

"I've run away from home... and I've nicked some chocolate."

"Where's home?"

"Small Heath, sir."

"Sir, eh?" The copper nodded, "Right then, want to tell me all about it?"

Mick did, all of it. His father's temper. His dream of reading plays and acting on the stage. The accusation of being a "poof." The shouting. The fear.

There were plenty of coppers who might've told him to bugger off, maybe even given him a clip round the ear to speed him home. But not this one. He listened, really listened, and even told Mick how he'd once run away at a similar age, terrifying his parents half to death.

He spoke of the dangers a young lad might face alone in the world. Not graphic, but clear enough that Mick understood, but for now he needed his parents' protection.

"Come on, let's get you home."

He muttered into a radio, and a few minutes later a marked Austin 1100 panda car pulled up. They drove to Small Heath, parking a couple of dozen yards from Mick's street.

"There you go, son. Think about what we talked about."

"Yes, sir. Erm...what about the chocolate bar?"

"Next time you get pocket money, pop back to the shop and say you forgot to pay. They'll appreciate it. Take care, lad."

The panda car pulled away and Mick watched it go, a little in awe of what had just taken place. In that moment, he knew what he wanted to be. He was going to be a copper. That was his future.

Nothing much changed at home. Mick continued growing up under a man who measured affection in the hardness of his handshake. He learned early how to read an expression, how to read a room, how to stay quiet, how to judge the distance between himself and danger, skills that would one day keep him alive. Small Heath wasn't an easy place for a gentle child to thrive, and under Dennis's roof, gentleness was treated like a disease.

By the age of twelve, Mick could fight. By fourteen, he knew when not to. And by sixteen, he'd realised the world was full of men like his father, loud, certain, and wrong, and that someone always had to deal with the mess they left behind.

School never held much glamour for Mick after that morning outside Digbeth nick. He still read everything he could get his hands on, Joyce on Monday, James Herbert by Wednesday, Shakespeare when he needed grounding, but classrooms felt too small for him. Too stiff. Too full of people who didn't know what the world was really like outside their front doors or so he assumed.

Teachers described him as 'bright but immovable', a lad who understood Macbeth better than the rest of the class put together but couldn't be persuaded to join the sixth form. He had his plan, fixed and unshakeable since the day a mustached constable had sat beside him on cold blue brick steps.

By the time he had turned fourteen, he was taller, leaner, and quicker than most boys in his year, a by-product of dodging his father's temper and absorbing his boxing lessons without absorbing his worldview. He wasn't a bully, and he didn't tolerate them either. More than one lad in the playground learned that Mick Dorrington's silence was not submission but calculation. He always struck last, and only if needed, and always with enough control that teachers whispered about "potential" rather than "trouble".

His talent for English, the essays, the literature, the way he could inhale a passage and breathe it back out word-perfect, made him an obvious target for Mr. Sanderson. "Call me Dave," insisted the young teacher with a past full of dusty costumes and half-forgotten walk-on parts at fringe theatres.

Dave badgered the Head until he wrangled permission for a school drama club, and Mick became his star recruit. It turned out the lad who'd grown up dodging his father's temper could slip into other skins with uncanny ease.

Bill Sykes in Oliver came first, all menace and swagger, and earned him more applause than he expected. Judge Turpin in Sweeney Todd followed, a role Mick played with such cold restraint that even some of the teachers shifted uneasily in their seats. But his peak performance, at least in Dave's eyes, arrived with Richard III. It was Dave who called it his pièce de résistance, pacing backstage with pride as Mick, fourteen, maybe fifteen, prowled the boards like a born villain.

Most of the parents in the audience didn't understand a word of the play, and the pupils cared even less. Their applause was polite, bored even. Bill Sykes's dramatic demise the year before, had won far louder cheers. But among the handful of staff who'd turned up to 'show willing', there was a quiet murmur of respect. The boy had something, presence, precision, a flicker of darkness he could summon like a tool. They didn't know it then, but Mick Dorrington would play versions of that role again and again in the years to come, but not on this kind of stage, rather one of reality in the world of true life.

At fifteen he bought his first motorbike, a second-hand Honda CB125 he'd saved for with Saturday jobs and holiday shifts in a grim little warehouse not far from where he lived. The bike was the closest thing to freedom he'd ever owned.

The first time he kicked it to life, the engine coughing into a steady buzz, he felt like he'd plugged himself into the world's main circuit. He practiced in the dead-end streets behind the terraces, stalling, sometimes falling, swearing, trying again.

Within months of turning 16, he passed his bike test at the first attempt, the examiner remarking that he 'rode like someone twice his age', which Mick took as a compliment until he realised it might've meant he was too cautious. He didn't care. The bike wasn't for show. It was an exit. A horizon-maker.

By seventeen he passed his car test too, though he never loved four wheels the way he loved two. A car was convenience; a bike was identity.

He left school the moment the rules allowed, but not without a pinch of regret he'd never have admitted out loud.

By then he'd become close to a girl from the drama group, the sort of closeness that teachers gossiped about in the staff room, whispering that young Dorrington might finally have found something capable of taming him. It had looked like it might get serious. Might have been something, too, if they'd wanted the same things. But she was staying on to do A-levels, full of talk about universities and futures that came with timetables and neat little plans. Mick had other ideas. Other needs, if he was honest. He never revealed his plans to anyone. His decision - nothing to do with anyone else.

His teachers shook their heads and tutted in disappointment, muttering about "wasted potential" and "a mind better suited to Shakespeare than shift work." His mother cried quietly into a tea towel, torn between pride and the fear that her boy was about to slip into the same grey struggle she'd watched consume his father. And Dennis Dorrington, never one to miss a moment to pronounce judgement, only grunted, "About bloody time he stopped swanning about with books and got a proper living."

Mick didn't argue. He never did. He just packed up his things, which didn't amount to much, and stepped out into a world that wasn't expecting him. Neither did he go to a factory or the building sites like half his mates.

He applied to join the West Midlands Police Cadets, and got in.

CADET LIFE WAS DESIGNED to prepare the right young people for afuture in the police force. Two years of blunt edges and sharp lessons. They drilled at dawn, marched until their legs ached, ran cross-country in the freezing rain, swam lengths in tiled echoing pools, and sat exams that tested everything from law to local geography.

There were mock accidents with fake blood, lots of fake blood, staged crimes with volunteer "offenders", usually older cadets, endless community service tasks, sweeping parks, stewarding events or helping in youth centres.

He completed his Duke of Edinburgh Gold Award, which included a residential project with the Ambulance Service.

Some cadets quit. Some coasted. Mick endured. He had toughness in him, the kind that didn't shout about itself. Instructors noted his refusal to give up, to show weakness, to ask for shortcuts. When one lad froze during a fire-safety exercise inside a smoke-filled training room, it was Mick who dragged him out by the collar. When an elderly man collapsed during a community event, Mick was the one who knelt beside him, talking softly until help arrived. Not heroic in the cinematic sense, just steady. Human. Present. And in the inner city rougher neighbourhoods of the city, he stood out. People talked to him. Not because he forced it, but because he listened. Because he understood fear without being frightened by it. Because he spoke quietly in places where everyone else tried to shout.

His instructors called it "rapport". Mick thought of it simply as reading a room, something he'd learned long before he put on a uniform.

He was also well-liked among his fellow cadets, the sort of chap everyone nodded to, joked with, invited for a pint, but no one ever really knew him. Mick had a knack for being present without being exposed, friendly without becoming familiar.

He trained hard, laughed in the right places, pulled his weight in every drill and duty, yet somehow remained slightly apart. A few of them later admitted they sometimes forgot he was one of them at all. He carried himself like someone older, someone who'd already seen a bit more of life than the rest. By the end of cadet training his assessments all read the same: resolute, instinctive, brave, unquestionably police officer material.

As expected, Mick joined West Midlands Police as a probationary constable in 1983. After completing his initial course at the regional training centre, followed by a local extended awareness procedure in Birmingham, fate dealt him a familiar card: his first posting was ironically at Digbeth Police Station.

He was allocated a room in the station's Single Men's Quarters, a narrow box room with thin walls, a single bed that creaked if you so much as breathed on it, and a wardrobe door that never quite closed no matter how you coaxed it.

The window looked out over the courtyard: grey brick, pigeon droppings, the occasional shout from a sergeant bawling out a probationer. To most people it would've felt like a cell with delusions of grandeur. To Mick, it felt like the top floor of the Savoy. He'd never had a space of his own before, not really. So he claimed it.

A couple of posters went up on the walls: Debbie Harry, who was quite often his imagined lover when he was in a certain sort of mood, and the holy trinity of his musical education; Led Zeppelin, Ozzy, Black Sabbath. With those faces watching over him, that little room became something precious. It wasn't luxury, but it was his. And for a lad from Small Heath, that meant more than feather pillows and fancy carpets ever could.

On his first day, before lining up for parade and presenting his appointments: truncheon, pocketbook, whistle, as required, and before meeting his sergeant and the rest of his unit, he walked outside and found the exact step he'd sat on as an eight-year-old.

He stood there for a moment, hands in his pockets, listening to the rumble of traffic along Digbeth High Street. Trucks transporting their cargo to the nearby abattoir to meet their fate. He would soon experience the odd escapee, sensing the worst and making a desperate bid for freedom. Pigs, sheep, cattle, it caused havoc. An old hand had told him that without exception they always ran down the hill away from the city, and Mick would soon learn that he was right. There's no supplement for experience.

He tried to picture the friendly giant in the blue serge uniform, the booming voice, the moustache, the kindness that had set the compass of his whole life. He'd never learned the man's name, never discovered what had become of him. But Mick hoped, wherever he was, he was still out there doing what good men do.

And with that quiet thought, he straightened his tunic, stepped inside, and began his career. The boy who'd once perched on the steps of Digbeth nick with a stolen chocolate bar in his pocket had crossed back over that line, not as a runaway but as a man finally stepping into the life he'd chosen.

A COUPLE of the old hands on the unit took it upon themselves to make sure Mick was 'made of the right stuff', as they put it, and that he learned the unofficial rules, the conventions that were never written down but enforced with a knowing smirk. Never rush to a domestic, no matter how bad the screaming sounds. Turn up too fast and you'll drag the husband out by his collar only to have the wife claw at your eyes for ruining their evening. Take your time and they'll have sorted it themselves, or passed out drunk, or both.

On nights, just before two in the morning, there was always some poor sod so bursting he'd christen a shop doorway. Nick him for 'disorderly conduct', and you'd be the one finishing at two so you could give evidence at Magistrates next day. "You'll do — off at two," was the mantra.

Never drag a vagrant out of a public toilet unless you fancied being sand-blasted for lice at the health station at Little Park Street. Better to move them along and leave the uniform free of infestation.

Mick listened to the pearls of wisdom, nodded in the right places, made mental notes, and quietly decided which lessons he'd ignore. If his mum were getting a hiding, he'd want coppers to get there fast. If he saw some bloke relieving himself in a doorway, he wasn't about to let that take him off duty - a short, sharp warning should suffice. And as for the vagrants, well, if they were sleeping somewhere the public, including his mum, might have to sit, he'd drag them in and they could get deloused together. But for now, he listened. Because listening was what was expected. He played the game.

The reports on Mick were good. Solid. His sergeant, Ronnie Ross, a rum old character who'd seen more of the world at 3 a.m. than most people see in a lifetime, took Mick out on his designated beat for half a shift. After a couple of hours he said, "You'll do," and let him off the leash.

There are cops who are good, and there are cops who are lucky. Mick seemed to be the latter. Right place, right time, again and again. A natural thief-taker.

One wet night, sheltering in a shop doorway and sneaking a quiet fag, he felt a pair of size nines drop onto his shoulders. A burglar had climbed out through the transom window, pockets stuffed with loose till cash and dragging a brand new Echo Blaster behind him, and had picked exactly the wrong moment to make his exit.

The lads from the Criminal Investigation Department were over the moon, not that they'd ever admit it. The Night Detective told Mick to "shove him in a cell," and they'd take over in the morning. The bloke confessed to a string of burglaries, and CID celebrated their victory with a bottle of Scotch, bought for themselves. Mick was given the generous compliment of being 'reasonably bright'.

Experiences kept rolling along. A month later he grabbed a chap trying to break into a motor behind Digbeth Station. Mick mentioned, almost casually, that the guy was a dead ringer for the photofit of an armed robbery suspect on the station wall. The detective, halfway through a phone call Mick suspected wasn't remotely police business, grudgingly came to look, and nearly fainted.

"Good lad," he muttered, "Right son, I'll take it from here."

Ronnie Ross made sure Mick got the credit that he deserved. CID weren't taking that away from him.

Then Special Plain Clothes, Vice, came knocking. They wanted a uniform who looked young and clean enough to pass for a punter. Ross introduced Mick to a bloke called Dave M, no surname offered, an initial had to do , a sergeant with a leather jacket, cowboy boots, and the sort of stubble that cost more than Mick's weekly wage.

"Michael,... Mick...., welcome to vice," Dave said, "Now go get into civvies. Jeans, tee-shirt, white if you've got one, tight as you can manage. Trainers. No socks. Slick your hair back. We've got a job."

Mick wasn't stupid. He could see what he was being set up for from the moment he heard the location: the public loos at Paradise Circus. A known 'cottaging' spot. Random locations, often public toilets where homosexual men might meet likeminded men for a brief casual sexual encounter were known as 'cottages'. It seems that the Lord Mayor had been approached after he had been taken short while he was in civvies, had moaned about it, and now Vice had to be seen to be doing something. Entrapment with a smile.

"Don't approach anyone," Dave warned. "Just stand there and look... available. If anyone tries it on, tap your nose. We'll do the rest."

Mick did as he was told. Four men , two of them married, all decent enough working men, were charged with importuning under the Sexual Offences Act. All pleaded guilty. Looking back, Mick would come to regret that afternoon deeply. But at the time, he got a letter of thanks from Dave, saying there'd be more work, better work, coming his way soon.

And Mick, despite the reservations he tried not to dwell on, was up for it. Because he knew one thing: he wasn't going to be a copper wearing a uniform for too long. He was made for the street. And the street would soon take notice.

Over the next couple of years, Mick spent more time in civvies than he ever did in uniform. The irony wasn't lost on him: the commendations pinned to his chest said police officer, but most days he looked more like the sort of lad the police liked to throw against a wall and search. His bosses didn't mind. His successes reflected well on them, too well, in some cases, and they were more than happy to keep him away from the front line as long as he kept producing results. And he did. Not just with Vice, either.

The Black Country is that region west of Birmingham city and widely regarded as an entirely different world to its adjacent neighbour, a little rougher, a little tighter, a lot more suspicious of strangers. But for reasons no one could quite put their finger on, Mick could walk into places where a white, clean-cut copper had no business being, and somehow people accepted him. Maybe it was the easy grin. Maybe it was the way he listened before he spoke. Or maybe it was because he looked like a lad who understood the rules of places that didn't trust rules. Even Mick found it hard to define.

A couple of times the regulars searched him, but the finger scales and the small block of resin he carried as props were enough to convince them he was sound. He mapped out the pubs and clubs for the Drugs Squad; who was selling, who was using, who was pretending not to notice either. When the raids came, Mick would be swept up with the rest, hands on the bonnet, knees on concrete, just another face in the crowd. Once the court cases were done and the dust settled, he often drifted back inside the very same venues. A nod here, a drink there, and the room forgot he'd ever been carted off in a police van.

The longer he stayed off the front line, the less he resembled the freshfaced probationer his superiors remembered from training. A year of dodgy pubs, cheap beer and cheaper cigarettes aged him faster than a decade of ordinary policing.

Then came the Vagabonds MCC, Birmingham's rough-and-ready motorcycle club, long before the Overlords MC took over the postcode.

In the hierarchy of motorcycling clubs, the outlaw clubs were the only clubs permitted to call themselves an MC (Motorcycle Club), they were also the only clubs permitted to wear the three piece back patch, known as 'colours', consisting of the 'top rocker", often the name of the club, a 'bottom rocker', often the district, area or country the club was located in, and a central club emblem.

Other clubs would only be allowed to call themselves MCC (Motor Cycle Club), and they would not wear the three piece back patch. To do so would risk getting some unwanted attention from the dominant outlaw MC in an area. That could get quite nasty.

In terms of membership, there were full club members, the highest being the 'President', and other specific roles, denoted by a front breast patch, such as 'Quartermaster' or 'Sergeant at Arms'. The military structure wasn't surprising given that most outlaw clubs were formed by former WWII US Veterans finding themselves unwelcome in their own country, having spent years together fighting to protect the world from fascism.

Other than the specific roles, there were ordinary club members, who wore the club colours. To become a full club member, you would start by going to venues where the club would meet, socialising and partying, until you were asked if you wanted to join the club. If you did, and none of the members objected, you would become a 'Prospect' and be allowed to wear part of the colours, but not the full logo. After that it was months, sometimes years, of proving your value to a club before you could be voted in as a full member. More recently, becoming a 'hangaround', the socialising part meant probably six months, maybe more, of drinking warm lager with lads who'd grown up in care homes and found their first taste of discipline in the rigid hierarchy of a back-patch club.

Mick blended in seamlessly: leather, denim, engine oil under his nails. He learned how they moved, how they drank, who they feared. He added a couple of tattoos, extra credibility. Eventually, he located the safe house where a full member, armed, volatile, and wanted for shooting a rival, was holed up. That tip got the man arrested, and almost got Mick killed.

After the bust, the Chapter held their own inquest, trying to sniff out the grass. Mick was summoned to attend. He kept his mouth shut, his pint steady, and his face unreadable. The Chapter President vouched for him almost immediately. Suspicion blew sideways, away from Mick and onto some poor sod who'd annoyed the wrong person.

He stayed on a little longer after that, until the Midlands Overlords MC swallowed up the smaller clubs, Vagabonds MCC included. The city's biker landscape changed overnight, and so did the risks.

Mick had proven himself well enough that the Overlords MC offered him the chance to "Prospect", the final step before becoming a fully patched member. It was as much a compliment as it was a warning. He turned them down with a neat little story about leaving the country for a lover. They bought it. Or they wanted to.

He broke off ties cleanly, but he knew what every undercover knows; the past never really goes away. You can only avoid old faces for so long in a town as tangled as Birmingham. Running into someone you'd once shared a drink with, or betrayed, or lied to, that was the game. You survived by thinking on your feet and keeping your ears open. By remembering who you were meant to be, before they asked. Undercover work wasn't about acting. It was about staying alive.

By 1989, Mick's work hadn't gone unnoticed. He was officially transferred to the Drugs Wing of the No. 4 Regional Crime Squad, based in the Midlands, a place that suited him far better than any high-visibility jacket or beat patrol ever had.

The Regional Crime Squads (RCSs) were police units, formed in the 1960's and 1970's to tackle organised crime across force boundaries in England and Wales. In due course, each RCS would also have a Drugs Wing, to tackle cross border drug trafficking.

Working in 4 RCS Drugs Wing suited Mick perfectly. When he wasn't under a false name in some backstreet pub, he was tucked into a surveillance van with a flask of lukewarm tea, watching doorways and curtains and the slow, inexplicable rhythms of criminal life. It kept him out of the way of ordinary policing, which everyone agreed was for the best.

When the Metropolitan Police's undercover unit, who were responsible for all undercover operations in England and Wales, offered West Midlands Police a couple of places on their prestigious National Undercover Course, Mick's name was the first written down. Someone joked that he'd probably been undercover before he joined the police, no one was entirely sure it was a joke.

Thirty men and women started on Mick's intake. Thirty good officers who could handle themselves, keep their stories straight and pass for ordinary people. But the training stripped more than half of them down to nerves and raw instinct; by the end, only ten remained standing. Mick was one of them. Not the toughest, not the loudest, just the one who kept his head when others lost theirs. Calm under pressure, able to think on his feet, and to turn any development into his own advantage.

Graduating the course meant that he was no longer just a local talent. He was now, officially, a national asset. The kind of operative who could be sent anywhere in the country, potentially even overseas, dropped into any environment, and trusted to breathe the air without raising suspicion.

He stayed on the Regional Drugs Wing, but the terms of his employment shifted. The bosses expected him to spend time, real time, building his legends. Backgrounds with weight. Histories that felt lived in. A flat here, a job there, a set of mates who knew him by a name that wasn't on any police payroll. Identities he could slip into at a moment's notice, as comfortably as shrugging on a battered leather jacket. At any given time he had one main pseudonym identity, ready to go, and two more in development. He wasn't just playing roles anymore. He was becoming them.

The next three years blurred into a carousel of short-term stings and throwaway identities. Mick drifted from one alias to another, a buyer here, a courier there, a nobody who happened to know somebody who could get hold of something. The work was quick, sharp, and dirty: buy-and-busts in backstreet boozers, controlled purchases of smack, charlie, wizz, ounces, kilos, sometimes multi-kilos. Enough gear to rattle cities. Enough evidence to make senior officers beam like proud uncles. He didn't just learn the trade; he absorbed it. Before long, he knew drugs the way a butcher knows cuts of meat, texture, smell, purity, price, who dealt what and how much a decent bit would fetch in Wolverhampton compared to West Bromwich or Bristol. He could tell Persian brown from Turkish just by rubbing a fleck between his fingers. He could tell the purity of cocaine using a glass beaker and a bottle of Domestos bleach. He became the man drug squad detectives rang when they needed to know whether a chalky wrap was worth a tenner or twenty-five to the right punter. But dope was only the start.

The Regional Crime Squad discovered that Mick's brain, when it liked a subject, locked on like a terrier. Soon he was knee-deep in forgery work, funny money, travellers' cheques, bankers' drafts, the whole crooked syllabus. He learned how a counterfeit note felt slightly too warm straight off the press, how the ink sat just a fraction too proud, how acetates were cleaned, stored, traded.

He recovered values into the multi-millions, the plates that printed them, and the acetates that were used to make the plates too. He worked all over the country. Wales, north and south, London, Geordie land in the northeast, Manchester, anywhere really, meeting counterfeiters who didn't trust a soul but warmed to him after two pints and a shared cigarette.

He slept in bedsits that stank of damp and cheap cooking oil, motels where the walls vibrated with the couple next door, and safe houses where the only sign of civilisation was a kettle with a broken lid. Occasionally he drove prestige cars and would casually throw the keys to the Valet Attendant of the boutique hotel he'd booked into. When he was in role, he was in role. He never switched off, even when he was alone. The mask stayed in place. He never knew who might be looking.

He was good at his job. Too good, some said. The kind of good that meant he no longer looked like a police officer pretending to be a criminal, he looked like a criminal pretending not to be.

Whenever he returned to the real world, he brought more tattoos with him. Those who knew him started to wonder what he had become.

Sometimes even Mick new that he needed to decompress. To have a complete break and remember exactly who he was. To spend some time being Mick Dorrington. To drive to see his parents without constantly looking in the rearview mirror. To live without having to dry-clean himself. To have a day to himself riding the lanes of Warwickshire on his latest steel machine

4

IN SICKNESS AND IN HEALTH

On a warm Sunday afternoon in the July of 1991, Mick was blowing a few cobwebs away tearing up the tarmac astride his black Kawasaki KZ1000 CSR, making his way through Henley-in-Arden, heading towards Stratford-upon-Avon. A few minutes by the river, chillin ", maybe a cold drink , just one, then heading home. No legends, no informants, no surveillance vans, just the road, the roar of the engine, and the rare luxury of not thinking about the job. The gentle roar from his pipes turned heads. He turned heads, He looked the part. You couldn't miss him, except when an old boy in an even older Jag did.

The vehicle lurched out of a side street straight into his path. Only yards in which to react. One of those 'sorry mate, didn't see you,' moments that bikers experience more often than they should. Most were rescued by the skill and experience of the biker. Mick flicked a glance to the opposite lane, oncoming traffic, packed tight. No escape route this time. Pavements were not an option. No time for anything except instinct.

This shit is going to hurt.

He slammed his brakes, trying to keep the wheels upright. The tyres screamed, the bike juddered, and then....crash.

He doesn't remember it.

Reality returned by degrees: the smell of scorched rubber, an ice cream cone melting on the pavement nearby and a small stream of sticky cream slowly dripping off the kerb near his head, funny what the senses notice in such moments, the sound of a sobbing child, or maybe it was a woman. Not sure. Three or four people circled him, staring down, wideeyed. Someone kept repeating, calm but urgent, that he'd had an accident, he knew, and needed to stay still. He wasn't going anywhere , not for a moment. Help was on the way.

Seconds, or was it minutes. He wasn't certain. A new voice broke through. Authoritative, clinical, confident.

"I'm Anna, I'm from the ambulance service. Can you tell me your name, please?"

Training flicked on like a switch.

Name? Which name? Who am I? Am I working? No. Not today. Day off.

"Erm, my name's Mick."

"Well, Mick, it looks like you've broken your left leg, quite badly. I need to check you for other injuries."

Only then did the pain make itself known, a deep, nauseating shock that surged through him like electricity. He couldn't help but let out a yelp.

"I'm going to give you a bit of morphine. It'll make you feel really good."

It did. The pain softened. The world felt even warmer. He was comforted by the drug. Another experience he'd log away for the future.

"We're taking you to Warwick Hospital. Is there anyone you'd lik eus to call?"

There wasn't, not yet. Maybe later.

They slowly lifted him into the ambulance with careful, practiced hands. Paramedic Anna stayed beside him, attractive, steady, the kind of presence he might have flirted with under different circumstances. But every nerve in his leg was screaming and charm wasn't an option. More morphine was given. Nice.

The next few hours dissolved into a blur of movement and white light. X-rays. Questions, answered and repeated too many times. Don't they write this shit down?

The clipped voice of a doctor explaining a tibial plateau fracture, something about a broken wrist, broken thumbs something about the sort of broken thumbs that skiers sometimes suffer.

Surgery under general anesthetic, that day, possibly, he wasn't sure. More morphine. Then the soft, inevitable pull of unconsciousness. And peace, the first he'd had in a while. He slept until they woke him to give him more medicine to help him sleep.

Morning always arrives way too early in a hospital. Even with the morphine fog still clinging to him, Mick heard the gentle scrape of curtains and a voice, familiar, soft, teasing, musical, coaxing him back to consciousness.

"Morning, it is you, Mick. I saw your name and thought, no... itcan't be, can it? But here you are. Mick Dorrington, the boy who stole my heart and then broke it in two." Playful. Not bitter. A light Irish lilt wrapped in brushed velvet. He'd once told her it was the sexiest voice on earth, and lying there half-drugged and half-broken, he realised he'd meant it.

He opened one eye, fighting the gluey weight of sleep.

"'Ello, Nancy me darlin'. 'Ave you been a good girl for your Bill?"

He slipped into that threatening mockney accent he'd once used when they were teenagers on stage together, Bill and Nancy, only now it actually sounded convincing.

She rolled her eyes but couldn't hide the smile. Same smile as ever. Same girl, only... older. More polished. A nurse's uniform instead of a school skirt. It suited her, made her look even .... sexier. Those green eyes still shone like emeralds, the red hair still managed to look like it was catching fire in sunlight. A dream surely, except he was awake.

Bernadette "Bernie" Connolly. The girl he'd been hopelessly in love with for eighteen solid months; the one who'd dumped him when she thought he wasn't taking their future seriously. She'd wanted A-levels, university, prospects and she wanted Mick by her side. He'd already decided on a police career, but he hadn't known how to say it, not properly, not then. She'd taken his secrecy for indifference, and by the time he'd worked out how to explain himself, it was too late. They had both moved on.

He'd regretted it more often than he had dared to admit. What about Bernie? Regrets? Had she married? Had kids? Moved somewhere in the country? He'd imagined her on and off for years, always with that laugh, always with that slight head-tilt she used to soften a scolding.

"Mick," she said, tucking a stray lock of red hair behind her ear, a gesture he remembered far too well, "I've got to go on my rounds. Doctors will be with you shortly. I'll pop by later, yeah? I'm dying to know what you've been up to. You look like You've collected a few stories."

She twirled away with the same light step she'd had at fifteen, sixteen maybe, a kind of skipping grace she couldn't have faked if she tried. Still slim. Still impossibly pretty. Playful mischief still evident, even from twenty feet away. A nurse's uniform can't ever have looked any better and...no wedding ring.

Mick watched her go, his head sinking back into the pillow.

No ring.

But then again, this was a hospital. Plenty of young, handsome doctors about. One of them must've staked a claim. Still... that smile.

For the first time since the crash, the pain in his leg wasn't the only thing on his mind.

MICK'S FATHER died in the spring of 1992, after eighteen months in a care home that smelled of urine and antiseptic. Vascular dementia had peeled Dennis Dorrington away layer by layer, leaving behind a man who looked like Mick's dad, but who looked at him like a stranger. There had been long periods when Mick had been a stranger.

Sometimes Dennis would brighten when Mick walked in, grinning with the warmth of old days. An hour later, as Mick stood to leave, Dennis would frown and ask, "Who are you again, lad?"

The first few times, it felt like a knife. Later, it felt like routine. And strangely, God knows how, those fleeting moments of gentleness, those small smiles that surfaced without the old judgement behind them, brought them closer than they'd ever managed when Dennis had been in full command of his wits.

Iris followed a year later. Lymphoma. Hospital curtains, hushed corridors, the slow scrape of time running out. In one of their last conversations she took his hand and told him she was sorry he'd never chased his dream of acting.

"You should've been on a stage somewhere, love," she whispered, the words catching in her throat, "You'd have been a great actor. Another Richard Burton".

Mick squeezed her fingers and gave her the easy lie, "Don't worry, Mom. Maybe acting was never really for me."

She didn't notice the small smile he let slip, the kind that hinted at an untold story she would never hear now. A story about the great roles he had played, and the ones still to come. Not on any stage, not under lights or to applause, but out there, on the streets, in the suburbs, in the shadows. The roles that really mattered.

25 AUGUST 1991. A little over a year after he'd woken up to the sound of Bernie Connolly's velvet-and-shamrock voice drifting through the hospital curtains, Mick Dorrington found himself standing in a hired dinner suit at The Grand Hotel in Birmingham, trying to look like the sort of man who belonged in gilt-edged surroundings. It was a wedding far more plush than anything his family would've dared to plan, but Bernie insisted that if they weren't going down the church route, much to her very large, very Catholic family's horror, they'd at least do the thing somewhere with a bit of swagger. And Mick? He'd have married her in a bus shelter if she'd asked, so the Grand suited him just fine.

Ronnie Ross had been floored when Mick asked him to be Best Man. In their line of work, you didn't collect many people you'd trust to stand next to you in public. But Ronnie was loyal, sharp, and more importantly, knew when to keep his trap shut. He took the job with a mixture of surprise and pride and delivered a speech that managed to be funny without incriminating anyone—an achievement in itself.

The reception was loud, warm, and messy in all the right ways. One hundred and twenty guests, thirty from Mick's side, some family, mostly friends, and the rest an invading army of Connolly's. Bernie's clan danced, drank, sang, argued, danced again, and charmed the hotel staff until the early hours. Mick's colleagues blended in better than expected; cops and Connolly's weren't all that different when it came down to reckless celebration. The newlyweds ended the night in the penthouse suite, too exhausted and too happy to care about the absurdity of it all.

His mum had smiled throughout the day, but anyone who truly knew her could see it for what it was: a painted smile. Months of watching her husband's slow, inevitable deterioration had worn her down in ways she would never admit aloud. She had loved Dennis in spite of himself, and now that he was gone, something in her had gone with him. She would never be truly happy again. Even the prospect of becoming a grandmother seemed to rest heavily on her narrow shoulders, as if it were one more responsibility rather than a blessing. Looking back, Mick would wonder if she'd already known, somewhere deep inside, that she wouldn't be around much longer, that she'd be following Dennis sooner rather than later.

'Perhaps that's why she's so bloody miserable', he had thought at the time, a private, guilty joke he would later wince at remembering.

The year leading up to that day had blurred past Mick like the crash that had nearly killed him. Seven weeks in Warwick Hospital. For some inexplicable reason, medical professionals seemed to delight in warning him that his injuries would have very long-term implications.

He had very clear memories of the Ward Sister at Warwick, who Mick christened, 'the Angel of Grim Truth', who never once called him by name. To her, he was 'the organ donor', like every other motorcyclist who'd limped through her ward over the years. Dark humour, maybe, but Mick respected it. Riders knew the stakes; one inattentive 'cage dweller' and you were another broken memory on the asphalt.

Bernie visited every day that she wasn't working the wards herself, bringing contraband biscuits and that sly grin that had melted him at sixteen.

Seven weeks were enough for both of them to realise the truth, they'd been idiots to let go the first time. There was a gravity between them, something stronger than youthful romance and far harder to ignore.

By the time the hospital discharged him, seven weeks to the day after the crash, with a limp that would serve him very nicely in undercover work, they were already planning their lives together.

There were still many more weeks of pain and discomfort. Hydrotherapy, then Physiotherapy, and a steady procession of medics warning him about arthritis like bookmakers predicting a dead cert.

Within six-months, they were sharing a rented flat in Knowle. A polite, tidy Warwickshire village that pretended it didn't notice the Connolly's dropping by like a travelling troupe. Close enough to Birmingham and Warwick for work, far enough out for them to pretend it was a fresh start.

Two months later, they were planning a wedding with embarrassing urgency. Bernie was pregnant. Their first child on the way.

For the first time in years, maybe ever, Mick Dorrington felt like he was moving toward something rather than running from it. Bernie felt exactly the same. In the months since Warwick, he'd told her more about his work than he'd ever shared with another living soul, by a very long chalk.

She listened, not with the wide-eyed fascination he got from rookie U/C's, as undercover police officers were often called, when he was coopted into helping with training on the Undercover Training Course, but with the steady gaze of someone who cared enough to worry.

She knew he loved the job. But she doubted that slipping into other people's skins, drinking in back rooms with men who'd kill you for looking at them wrong, or spending time with "the wrong sort of women ", was the foundation on which happy marriages were built.

She wanted that marriage with Mick, more than anything. And when he told her he wanted it too, she believed him. For once, he wasn't dancing around the truth or hiding behind bravado. She mattered to him more than anything.

So he made her a promise, spoken quietly but with a weight that settled between them like a pact signed in ink. He'd return to work, finish his attachment with "the Regional," and then step away from the covert world. Look for a different posting. Something above board. Something safer. She didn't need to press him; he meant every word.

And for the first time since they were kids, there was nothing, no secrets, no doubts, to stop them binding their lives together.

His bosses were more cautious. Men like Mick didn't grow on trees, and they weren't thrilled about losing him. But a good officer with a limp and a pregnant wife was best handled carefully. So, when he returned to duty they eased him back through surveillance team, civilised hours, regular shifts, no covert meetings in dodgy venues. Bernie was delighted. Any lingering nerves she'd carried about marriage dissolved with each evening he walked through their flat door at a reasonable time, tired but intact.

Their honeymoon, a week on the Greek island of Kefalonia, felt like something borrowed from a different life altogether. Heat, wine, just the odd glass for Bernie, a warm, clear blue sea, and the sort of Greek food that only tasted good while in Greece. For seven days they were simply Mick and Bernie again: sun-tanned, unhurried, and quietly besotted with each other. Bernie caught him more than once gazing at her gently emerging bump, half wonder, half disbelief that life could ever be this generous. It was the sort of week that made a future feel not just possible, but inevitable. Sadly, life had other plans.

The sixth of February 1992, two-thirty in the morning: Emma

entered the world kicking and screaming. The midwife at Birmingham Women's Hospital, who bore a remarkably uncanny resemblance to the shock rock singer, Alice Cooper, had barely left Bernie's side through the seven long hours of labour. She had listened to Bernie's blistering critique of her husband, delivered in the sort of language that would have made a miner blush, and had taken it all in her unflappable stride. Then came the final push, the sudden slackening of pain, and the first, furious cries of their daughter. Bernie gathered the tiny, wrinkled creature to her chest, pressed her lips to the damp bloody swirl of scalp, and whispered, warm and breathless, "Oh, your fuckin' arsehole of a daddy is going to love you."

Mick cried when he arrived two hours later. He cried because he was late. He cried because he was happy. He cried because he was sorry. He cried because he had broken a promise to Bernie, and because he could already see in her tired smile that she had forgiven him.

Mostly, he cried because he didn't deserve either of them. And in that quiet, exhausted moment, he made himself another solemn vow: nothing like this would ever happen again.

But deep down—even then—he knew better than to make promises he couldn't keep

5

ON A CAROUSEL

Before Emma had made her appearance and while Mick's skin still held a trace of Greek sun, he turned up at the Regional Crime Squad Office in Bournville, expecting another week of the usual. Long hours half-asleep in battered cars, punctuated by occasional adrenaline spikes while tailing some career criminal nipping out for groceries or grabbing a bag of chips.

Surveillance could be dangerous, even exhilarating, but mostly it was mind-numbing in a way that only months of staring at the back of a suspect's semi-detached could teach you. Then, once in a blue moon:

Strike! Strike! Strike!"

Crash, bang, wallop. Villains in cuffs. Commodity recovered, sometimes. Then celebratory pints of lager afterwards. Except Mick was never on the strike team. He was the ghost in the wings. And that was how it had to be.

Detective Inspector Jonas Peters spotted Mick as he passed by his office. Mick liked Peters, a decent boss who knew when to give Mick room and when to watch for the cracks that came with the job.

"Mick, got a minute?"

He did. And he knew that tone. A job needed doing, his kind of job.

"You know Rhys Evans at Eight, don't you?"

Mick did. He'd done a couple of small walk-on parts for Detective Inspector Rhys Evans, No. 8 Regional Drugs Wing, testing coke purity during 'buy-and-busts' before everything went tits up for the villains. Rhys had rated him far more than Mick thought he deserved.

"Rhys has something bubbling. Says it's right up your street. He'll want you to spend a bit of time on it, if you're up for it. John Wall has the details."

Detective Sergeant John Wall, the ROSS - Regional Operational Support Sergeant for No. 4 Regional Crime Squad. Gatekeeper for every undercover deployment in the region. Keeper of pseudonyms, legend logs, car allocations, and the countless tiny details that stopped undercover jobs turning into preventable clusterfucks.

Good at his job, no question, even if he and Mick didn't entirely see eye to eye. Wall had once refused to release Mick for an under-cover operation in the U.S., sending his favoured mate instead, and it had gone to rat shit. Mick had never quite forgiven him.

Wall laid out the bones; a South Wales drug trafficker had vanished. Rumour was he'd been killed by a rival, a member of a local motorcycle club, but local enquiries had hit a wall. Rhys wanted Mick to take a run at it. A meeting had been set for Severn View Services the following Friday.

Wall unlocked a metal cupboard and handed Mick a familiar folder: Micky Robinson, his established biker pseudonym. Then an envelope, thick and soft with cash.

"Five grand. Rhys isn't cutting corners. Get yourself a clean set of wheels and any props you need. And..." the sergeant produced a smaller box before continuing, "there's some bling from our friend in the Jewelry Quarter, look after it."

No questions. No check-ins. No 'are you ready to work again? Are you ready to ride again?' No need. They both knew what Mick's answer would have been. Mick also knew that there was more to this job than had been let on. Maybe John Wall hadn't been fully briefed either. Maybe Rhys Evans had figured that he wouldn't get Mick if he'd given them the whole story. For now though, Mick had a few clear days to 'get into character' and to pick up his ride.

THE KNUCKLEDUSTER GOLD rings were unmissable, four squat blocks of metal that flashed like warning signs every time Mick flexed his fingers. So too the thick gold chain that wasn't meant to sit neatly beneath his oilwashed T-shirt, but to lie heavy and visible, like a mayoral badge of office beneath his now shoulder length, greased back hair. Vintage, oil-stained jeans hung low on his hips, and the cowboy-style biker boots were worn and scuffed at the toes. His leather jacket was scarred with road rash: long, pale abrasions across the sleeves where it had hit tarmac more times than he cared to remember. No back-patch now, no club colours... but there had been once. The ghost of it still clung to the cut. Anyone who knew the world would see it. A rubber wristband hung from a strap on the jacket, the Biker & Blues Festival, and another faded festival band sat tangled beside it. A couple more were too worn to decipher. Between them they whispered of biker festivals, drag strips, loud music, cheap beer, and biker girls wearing "PROPERTY OF—" patches with a sort of fierce pride.

All of it was just set dressing though. Props. Costume. What mattered, what sold the lie, was the man inside it.

Mick had spent enough years drinking with, watching, and in some cases living among outlaw bikers to know exactly how they walked, how they stared, how they laughed, how they kept their hands loose at their sides until they didn't. He'd met the men who could manufacture amphetamine in a shed, shoot a rival in a pub car park, and then raise thousands for a children's cancer fund without ever seeing a contradiction. Many clubs insisted that members behave impeccably in public, and most did. But even at their most polite, there was always that unmistakable whiff of a threat. Something you felt before you saw.

That was the scent Mick carried now. He wasn't pretending to be a biker. In the ways that mattered, he was one. He would soon be used to people going out of their way to avoid him.

The black Suzuki Intruder 1400 parked outside told Rhys Evans that Mick, or rather Micky Robinson, was already at the services. The bike wouldn't have been Mick's first choice. It was an import, a couple of years old, but it looked the part. The previous owner had modded it within an inch of its life: a salvaged Harley Fat Bob tank, lower capacity but meaner looking, a black respray that wasn't factory, forward-control foot pegs, ape hanger bars, leather panniers, and iron-cross mirrors.

It rode heavy at low speeds and cried out for the fifth gear that Suzuki finally added to the '90 model.

And the seat? Christ. If Mick had to ride it for long he'd need a new one before his spine gave out.

The dealer had spun him the usual story, enthusiastic owner, nervous wife, ultimatum, the bike or her, one of them had to go, you choose.

Mick didn't care. Three and a half grand changed hands, the dealer was delighted, and John Wall had soon arranged the paperwork for the ride to be registered to the Coventry address belonging to one Micky Robinson.

As soon as Mick spotted Rhys striding across the car park, he instinctively knew this job wouldn't be a quick in-and-out. There was weight to it. Duration. Something that needed patience and craft.

At least Rhys had dressed down: leather jacket, dark jeans, nothing to scream "copper". Mick gave him the briefest nod and, without breaking stride, palmed him an old envelope, the unused balance of the five grand, passing it the way villains passed cash in films. Subtle, but not too subtle. A handful of people milled around, but nobody paid attention. And if anyone did, and if anyone happened to know that Rhys Evans was a police detective inspector, Mick could later explain it away as giving him a bung. A payoff. A quiet favour. Easy. And just like that, the stage was set. Micky

Robinson was back in the world. And Mick Dorrington had evaporated into thin air...again.

THERE WAS this strange rhythm to the life Mick had chosen, if chosen was the right word. 'Fallen into' was closer to the truth. Every undercover or U/C learned the beat of it eventually.

When you were idle, you craved the next job like a man craves a smoke after a long shift. The phone would ring, and suddenly you were useful again, needed even. An operational head would explain the plan in the sort of vague outline that told you they didn't understand undercover work anymore than they understood rap music. Some admitted as much. Some didn't. And it never mattered anyway, because the job you got was never quite the job you'd been sold.

Once the briefing was done, the familiar dance began, negotiations, compromises, the quiet but necessary tug-of-war: what Mick needed to stay safe and credible versus what the seniors thought he would be able to "get away with". Often budget restrictions trumped common sense.

Then came the operation itself. No two were ever the same. Some were slow burners; some were all danger and adrenaline; some were long stretches of nothing where you forgot who you were supposed to be and who you actually were. But they always, mostly always anyway, came to a head.

The day the trap was sprung and on that day, houses were raided, villains cuffed, evidence bagged, instructions shouted over radios, everyone with a badge running on caffeine and applause. The team buzzed with that manic, punch-drunk triumph that came after weeks or months of tedium and frustration. Bosses congratulated their teams and themselves, and they phoned more senior bosses to break the good news and to receive more congratulations.

Meanwhile, the U/C, Mick maybe, or whoever, would be in some tired pub miles from the centre of the storm, nursing a pint they didn't really want and trying to make it last another half hour. They'd sit in a corner, listening to the fruit machine bleeps, waiting for some-one...anyone...to remember they existed.

Only a few hours before, they'd been the most important person in the operation. Now? Now the "proper police work" had begun they were no longer needed.

Naturally, eventually someone would turn up, breathless, offering a quick handshake, a "nice one, mate," and then disappear again because there were people to brief and reports to write and a thousand other things more pressing than the person who'd walked the tightrope for them.

Then the job was over. The adrenaline drained. And the U/C would find themselves staring at an empty glass, already waiting for the next phone call, the next briefing, the next identity to slip into. It was a cycle, as predictable as the tide. But there was nothing quite like it in the world.

AFTER RHYS HAD GIVEN MICK—MICKY—THE details of 'Operation Pancake', he'd offered that familiar line every U/C heard sooner or later, "How do you think we should do this?" Which, in the secret dialect of operational briefings, really meant: 'We've tried everything we know, it's all gone belly-up and you're the last card we've got left'.

Not that things were as straightforward as that. They rarely were. And Pancake, ridiculous name, chosen at random by the ROSS sergeant flicking through that battered list of operational titles, was already a mess before Mick ever set foot near it. When he'd taken the job, no one had bothered to mention that two previous attempts at an undercover approach had already gone spectacularly wrong. Only later did the truth seep out.

The first attempt had used a police informant, a grass clinging to the hope of shaving years off an impending sentence, acting as an "access agent." His job had been to introduce a U/C to the target, to reference them, say that they could be trusted, and then step back and pray it all came good. Instead, a few days after the introduction, they found him dumped in Bute Park, a stone's throw from Cardiff Central. Unconscious. Barely alive. Someone had scrawled the Welsh word 'hysbyswr' across his forehead in thick red ink. Informer. Crude, but effective. The message landed. The U/C was told that he could stand down. He wouldn't be needed. Maybe there was another way.

The second effort took a different tack. Instead of using an access agent, the decision was made to attempt a straight infiltration.

The main subject, a biker who'd pulled together a small local club, wasn't patched yet, but the intentions were obvious enough. He wanted affiliation with one of the outlaw crews. Recognition. Legitimacy. A pathway to the mother club. And until that happened, he and his little collective met regularly at a pub on the outskirts of Cardiff, acting like they were already the real deal. Mick knew the U/C they'd chosen for the job... Rosie.

She'd put in her time in the shadows of the undercover world, on the arms of male colleagues, adding weight to their legends, smoothing over social gaps that men alone couldn't always bridge. She was good. Better than good. Rosie was the sort who could make heads turn without even trying, especially in leathers. And because she'd lived as much of the biker scene as she'd worked, she didn't need to study how to blend in; it was already written into the way she moved, talked, laughed.

They built the scenario around her strengths, mapped it out, rehearsed it, refined every beat until even Mick had to admit it had looked solid. In theory, at least, it should have stood a chance. Clean. Natural. Nothing forced.

Rosie had a perfectly legitimate reason to call in at the pub: she was waiting for a friend who hadn't shown. They had a plausible backstory, a logical reason for meeting there, and an equally logical excuse for why the friend had failed to appear. By the following morning, the local radio and papers would run a brief item about a motorcycle accident that had temporarily closed the M4, an appeal for witnesses, neatly tying off the loose ends. It was no problem actually closing the motorway for an hour or so. No theatrics, no unnecessary brushstrokes, just enough truth in the lie to give it texture.

The plan was simple. Rosie would wait outside long enough to make the delay credible, pacing, checking her watch, the picture of mild worry. Eventually she'd go inside and ask to use the pub's phone — concerned, apologetic, the way people get when they're asking for a favour from strangers. Maybe someone had heard about a crash. Maybe someone knew something she didn't. Just enough vulnerability to invite attention. Certainly someone would have heard about the motorway being closed. Attention, in that place, from that crowd, was guaranteed. Usually unwanted. Usually the wrong kind. But precisely the kind they needed.

Once she was inside, the rest would rely on her instincts. She'd stay visible, stay memorable, drip-feed just enough personality into the room to lodge herself in the subject's peripheral vision. Not forcing anything. Just a presence. A stranger who might, if the universe tilted the right way, become familiar. Gradually, subtly, she would ease herself into the subject's consciousness. That was the idea, anyway but it just never went like that.

Rosie arrived at the pub at the expected time, the engine tick-ticking as it cooled. Unseen eyes watched from the builder's van with the reflective privacy windows parked at an angle that wasn't quite natural. A radio crackled, "Eyeball, eyeball, confirming 'Juliet One is in situ."

The Traffic Branch had closed a section of the M4 in both directions, and blue lights could be seen from distance. Gantries flashed up warnings of an accident ahead. Perfect.

But before Rosie - 'Juliet One' - had even swung her leg fully off the bike, the subject casually strolled out of the pub, like he'd been expecting her. He didn't hesitate; he walked straight up to her. Rosie removed her helmet, shaking loose that long, curly mahogany hair, the kind that made half the job easy and the other half dangerous. Her eyes stayed soft, natural. Not a flicker to betray recognition.

The observation team recorded the timing: less than a minute. A few quiet words. A shift of posture. Nothing dramatic.

Then Rosie put her helmet back on, turned the key, and rode away.

The subject raised a hand in a lazy wave, more farewell than threat, and wandered back inside. He shook his head, amused or disappointed, hard to say.

The radio supplied a running commentary.

Later, in the debrief with Rhys, Rosie reported exactly what the subject had said, word for word.

"We don't welcome coppers in here, no matter how gorgeous they might be."

She'd tried to push back, keeping her tone light, almost playful.

"I don't have a clue what you're talking about arsehole..." But he cut straight through her line.

"Of course you do. I Don't want to have to fall out with you, so off you go before I start to lose my patience."

And then she saw them: two heavies easing into position just behind him. Not speaking. Not posturing. Just there. The faintest hint of a bulge at each waistband—subtle, but unmistakable. She didn't need a second invitation. No time for heroics. As the old song goes: 'You've got to know when to hold 'em, You've got to know when to fold 'em.' Fold.

She rode away, pulse hammering against the inside of her jacket, the operation already dead in the water.

And when Rhys had finished recounting the night's events, Mick knew, just as Rosie had known instantly, and Rhys had come to suspect, there was only one explanation: the job had been blown by someone who was supposed to be on the side of the good guys.

Mick could have walked away from the job there and then. No U/C was ever forced to take on an operation they weren't comfortable with. He wasn't going to do that, not immediately. So, exactly how did Mick think that 'we' should do this? Mick looked Rhys directly in the eye, "Do you trust me?"

"Of course".

"No, do you really trust me? Do you trust me enough to give me a free reign on this?"

"I do."

Mick could hear the hesitancy in the reply.

"Look," he continued, "Go back and tell your guys that Operation Pancake is pulled. If there's someone senior you can trust, properly trust, get them on board and shut it down cleanly. Let your lot crack on with whatever else they've got bubbling." He paused, then laid down the real terms.

"And this is how it's going to proceed."

Mick went through the conditions one by one, slowly, deliberately, making sure Rhys understood each before moving on.

He would be operating entirely alone. No cover team. No surveillance. No comms. No admin. Nothing. Total isolation.

If he needed expenses, flash money, kit, anything at all, it would be handled through John Wall at No. 4.

Rhys would speak to Wall, and Wall only, from now on. Any meetings between Mick and Rhys would be arranged through Wall as well, but never inside 8 Region. Not once. Not ever.

Absolutely no one else in Rhys's patch was to know anything was happening.

Most senior officers would have shut him down at "no cover team." Rhys didn't. Mick clocked that—and was quietly impressed.

Finally, he confirmed the last point. No one in Rhys's region knew the name Micky Robinson; no one yet knew that another U/C had been lined up. Good. He could keep the identity. And the Suzi. He just needed a new seat.

THE SUBJECT of Operation Pancake was Owen Jenkins, a thirty-two year-old from a long-established Newport family.

Intelligence reports on him had stacked up for years. On paper he looked like a minor league two player, A couple of low-level assault convictions, one for possession of dope another for handling stolen goods. Nothing that hinted at any scale. But every credible source, informant, and rival dealer had indicated that Jenkins was the primary supplier of amphetamine sulphate in Wales, parts of the Midlands, and most of the southwest.

He was running a production and distribution network capable of shifting industrial quantities. He'd been on the fringes of Overlords MC Wales for years, a 'hangaround' who, for reasons no one could quite explain, had never made the step up to prospect.

Mick found that odd; the club didn't usually hesitate when it came to recruiting useful men. Instead, sometime in the mid-eighties, they'd let Jenkins form a local club around Cardiff.

Not a back-patch outfit, but close enough, members wore the small S.O.M.C. patch ("Support Overlords Motorcycle Club") on the right breast, that was compulsory, with an R.B.O. patch ("Recognised By Overlords") if members had earned it. The understanding was simple: they would operate as a support club for the Overlords MC.

Overlords members dropped in on Jenkins regularly, and he donated generously—obscenely—to keep their favour. Meanwhile Jenkins himself was getting pretty rich. And his reputation, in certain circles, was that of a man who protected his business with absolute ruthlessness.

A couple of sources had talked about the disappearance of a smalltime Cardiff dealer, Alfie Giles, who had one day been hawking cut-price whizz, and the next he was gone. The rumours were that he'd crossed Jenkins, nothing dramatic, but enough to make himself a problem. And then he had disappeared. The implications were that Jenkins had ordered a hit on him or had done the business himself. Without a body, the police had little to go on.

The wheels in Mick's head were working overtime. Maybe this wasn't going to be as difficult as he'd first anticipated. No not difficult, but not quick. This was going to take a long time to progress, but there would be benefits along the way.

When Mick ran the idea past John Wall, his verdict was about as warm as a tyre iron.

"You're fucking insane, you'll do fine."

Then Wall opened his secure cupboard, swapped one set of false documents for another, and slid across a neat folder stamped Michael James Dee.

Micky Dee wasn't new. He'd first been born out of the Vagabonds job a good eight years earlier...a ready-made biker who'd 'moved abroad for love' when things got too hot.

Mick had never taken up the Overlords 'Prospect' offer back then; he'd used the exit story and walked. But he'd kept the persona alive in the drawer, passport, credit cards, a life on paper, just in case.

Well, the case had come around where 'just in case' mattered. Now Mick needed Micky Dee back. He needed to see whether a narrative of 'unexpected life events' would carry him back into the Overlords orbit in Brum, to hang around for a while, be vouched for, to Prospect, to get closer, step by step, inch by inch, to where the real work waited.

Don't get ahead of yourself, Mick. One move at a time. This was going to be a long job, not days and weeks, but months, many months probably, maybe even years. At some point in the future Mick would look back at 'Operation Carousel' with a lot of sadness, rather than what should have been immense pride.

Micky Dee drifted back into the Overlords MC orbit the way a stray dog finds its old yard—half hopeful, half expecting a boot. He walked into one of their Birmingham haunts and was clocked almost instantly by two fully-patched members he recognised from the old Vagabonds MCC days. Same men, same scars, but the eyes... those were different now. Harder. Colder. Eyes that had stared down too much trouble and sent some of it to an early grave.

They recognised him straight off, and, Christ help him, they were pleased to see him. Bought every word of the story he fed them about the woman he'd loved dying slowly and painfully somewhere far from home. The crucifix tattoo with her name inked beneath it sealed the deal.

Grief always plays well in these circles; it's the one currency nobody wants to touch but everyone respects. The tale of him drifting back to Brum, picking up a Fat Boy, seeing who was still alive or out of prison, it all made sense to them.

So they welcomed him back. A ghost from the past with biking in his veins and no colours on his back. He could ride with them, drink with them, laugh with them, but there were doors he couldn't walk through, secrets he wasn't privy to. Fine by Mick. That suited the job, and it suited the part of him that still clung to home.

They asked him, more than once, if he was ready to become a Prospect. It would've been easy to say yes. Too easy. And if he did, he'd be chained to them, every dirty job, every sleepless night, every unwritten rule.

Prospects weren't club members, they were tools used by the full members. So he played it coy. "Thinking about it," he'd say, nursing a beer, acting the man torn between freedom and belonging.

But time doesn't stand still for undercover men. It grinds them down. By the time he could no longer stall, he'd already missed Emma's birth. Bernie, heavy with their second, was running out of patience, and Mick knew it. She didn't say much, not anymore. That was how he knew he was truly in trouble. And then came the hammer blow.

Unanimous approval. Micky Dee, Prospect of Overlords MC. They presented him with his new patches: the top rocker screaming Overlords, the bottom one marked Prospect, the little MC patch that told the whole world exactly who he was riding with. These weren't bits of cloth, they were chains disguised as colours.

From that moment on, Mick was theirs. Guarding bikes in piss-stinking alleys while the patched boys drank and whored inside. Running errands that no one with any pride would touch. Sleeping odd hours in odd places. Stinking of petrol, sweat, and other Men's expectations. Seeing less and less of Bernie and Emma until his family life felt like a dim memory. And still he told himself it was for their safety, and that the distance protected them. Now he had to bring the next part of the plan to life. No turning back. Not now.

It was a couple of the patched lads who'd first clocked the woman at the Rock and Blues Custom Show, a four-day haze of fumes, booze and bad decisions up at Pentrich, Derbyshire. One of them nudged Mick with a greasy thumb and that sly grin they all wore when trouble walked into view.

"Oi, Virus," one of them barked, the nickname had stuck the moment someone joked he'd come back from the dead like a bad infection, "There's a bird over there gaggin' for it. Looks like she's after a virus, Virus."

The laughter came thick and stupid. It always did. But the scene that followed looked natural enough—too natural, which was the point.

Erin drifted into view with the easy swagger of someone who'd grown up scraping her knees on rock and shale. Welsh valleys in her voice, London edges in her eyes.

Seven years in the Met had taught her how to stare down the wrong sort of man, and a lifetime on off-road bikes meant the leather and engine oil suited her more than most of the blokes in the field.

No one knew she preferred women. No one needed to. It simply meant she could play the part without ever losing herself to the performance. And people liked Erin, couldn't help themselves. That helped more than any forged ID ever could.

From there, it was stepping stones—tiny shifts in routine, small dramas acted out with the air of spontaneity. A drink shared. A joke tossed between them. A silent look held too long under festival lights. Bit by bit, Virus and Erin, 'Property of Overlords MC' as her patch eventually declared, became a fixture. A unit. Something the club didn't question.

For a month or two it held. Then came the wobble, the slow, believable ache of homesickness. Wales pulling at her like a tide. She missed the hills, she said. Missed the sound of people who spoke the way she did, she said. It rang true enough for the Overlords to humour her. Meetings were arranged. Voices lowered. Deals struck in smoke-choked rooms. And eventually, with a nod from the right man in the right moment, Mick was accepted as a Prospect for the Overlords MC Wales chapter.

What continued was the grind of Prospect life, long hours, longer silences, and the sort of jobs designed to wear a man down. But Mick endured it, because he had to. Because Bernie and the kids were already slipping into the fog of things he didn't have time to hold onto. Because the shadows were closing in and he'd chosen to walk into them anyway.

Weeks blurred into months. The club hardened around him. Trust was earned the slow, painful way: pints drained, secrets traded, nights guarding bikes in rain that cut sideways.

Until eventually, inevitably, he was given a new task. Collect envelopes. Small ones. Heavy with cash. Collect them from Owen Jenkins. A man no one in the club cared for, not really.

"Jenkins wants in," one of the patched members muttered to Mick, handing over a note and a smirk, "But we can't stand the prick. Don't tell him that. Just string him along. Let him think he's got a chance of getting patched. That's your job now, Virus. You're his mate. His contact. Have fun."

And so he did the runs. And Jenkins talked. Boy, did he talk. Money, product, ambition that stank of chemicals and arrogance. He liked Virus. Trusted him even.

One night over cheap beer, Jenkins leaned back, eyes shining with the fever of his own genius. "You'll be even more impressed when you see my lab running full tilt," he said. "You can tell your boys I could make them ten times what they're pulling now."

And that was it. The moment the trapdoor shut. The point beyond return.

～

AT 1 P.M. on 14 June 1995, Operation Carousel finally staggered toward its grim conclusion. Rhys Evans sat in the back of the unmarked van, nerves jangling, watching the Midlands boys check and re-check their weapons with the calm of men who do this too often. They hadn't told him where they were going...didn't need to know...but he was the only local face who knew the name attached to the target.

He'd been caught off guard by John Wall's phone call the previous Friday; the man was brisk, almost cheerful, as if ordering sandwiches instead of a cross-border strike. Rhys was to gather a small Welsh team, no questions, no chatter. They were 'helping the Midlands with something'. Everything about the job felt sealed-off and scorched-earth, the kind of operation where names got filed away in locked drawers and left there.

When the church bells marked the hour, the hammer dropped. Three addresses, three doors kicked in with military precision, the air filled with splintered wood and the metallic bark of shouted commands. Guns, dogs, detectives, an organised storm overwhelming the small pockets of crime that had wrongly thought themselves to be invisible and untouchable.

The factory, a lonely farm cottage barely two miles from where Erin had once rode her tiny trails bike as a child, was the centre of it. Someone had remarked that it looked like a twisted version of Snow White and the Seven Dwarfs, reimagined as sweating, dead-eyed men churning out soaking-wet amphetamine sulphate on a production line slick with chemical stench. At the far end, "Grumpy" was sealing up vacuumpacked kilos, still dripping, still pure, the kind of stuff that didn't just ruin lives but hollowed out whole towns.

And presiding over the chaos stood Jenkins. He and two of his hired knuckle-draggers, likely the same pair who'd bullied Rosie out of the pub, held handguns in trembling fists. But when three Heckler & Koch MP5 automatics are staring you down, even bravado has its limits. They dropped their weapons like men waking from a nightmare.

Evidence teams swarmed; every bag, every beaker, every note of scribbled chemistry was swallowed into brown-paper custody. Bagged and tagged.

The terraced house on the outskirts of Cardiff offered a different kind of truth, empty rooms, stale smoke, the faint smell of damp soaked into the walls. But the detectives found what mattered: ledgers, bank statements, and £25,000 in crisp notes confirmed by a humming bank-note counter that had been helpfully left by the occupants.

The last address in Newport gave up something darker still: a bin beside an outhouse containing clothes half burned and half stained with blood, an indecisive attempt to erase a crime committed too hastily to hide. They were already rotting. Why hadn't someone got rid?

Days later, after Rhys replayed scraps of drunken confession Jenkins had spilled to Mick, he requested a search near Garth Hill. A place of wind-worn grass and sheep tracks, near Pentrych, a landscape popular with hikers.

It was a sniffer dog that found the patch of disturbed undergrowth, nosing at the earth like it had been taught if it wanted a reward. They uncovered what remained of Alfie Giles; barely a body, more a patch of biology and DNA, laid shallowly in the soil. Bullets Don't rot. Forensics descended, swarming over the taped off hillside like ants.

Meanwhile, at about 12:55 p.m., as blue-lights were about to converge on Jenkins's kingdom, Mick rode away from the makeshift lab with the quiet finality of a man closing a door he'd never thought he'd open.

His work was done; the persona of Virus could start to dissolve, flake away like dried mud. The Overlords would grieve him in their own roughhewn way, once the papers printed the tale of a lone biker coming off his machine on a rain-slick bend, sometime after lunch on the fourteenth of June. Tragic, they'd call it, shaking their heads as if tragedy wasn't the natural end of men like him. His colours would go up in the clubhouse, black leather stiff with road dust, the name VIRUS stitched above a chest pocket like a warning or a punchline. They'd pin them to the wall beside the others who'd ridden too hard, too far, and too close to the edge. A toast, a few muttered stories, and that would be that. The world moves on, even when it shouldn't.

No one spared a tear for Jenkins. The news of his arrest barely caused a ripple.

"Bloke was a complete fanny—fuck him," the President said, wiping ale from his beard, and that was the club's final word on the matter.

If there was any real feeling, it was for the lost income, the steady drip of easy cash that had sweetened their mouths. Money is mourned longer than men, in outfits like theirs.

And somewhere beneath it all was the sense that things had unfolded exactly the way they were inevitably going to. Mick's death, Jenkins's fall, the club shrugging off both like last week's weather. In the end, inevitability has a way of tidying up after itself.

Nine months later, Cardiff Crown Court, and Owen Jenkins finally faced the long shadow he'd been running from. The man who'd swaggered through back rooms and lock-ups now looked like a broken man. When the charge of manslaughter was put to him, he croaked out a guilty plea. His brief rose, a macabre little puppet, talking about an "accidental shooting"— twice—panic, fear, poor judgement, remorse. It all spilled out like cheap gin: thin, insincere, and reeking of desperation.

The Judge listened, stone-faced, hands folded as if in prayer to some God who'd long since abandoned the Welsh courts. He nodded at the mitigation, accepted the performance for what it was, a necessary ritual, and then lowered the hammer. Twenty years. Even with the concurrency for the drug charges, it might as well have been a lifetime. Jenkins flinched only once when the court clerk read out the full list of seizures. £128,000 stripped from him in clean, clinical strokes of law. Three properties taken too; homes turned into forfeited trophies. You could almost hear the last of his imagined empire collapsing in on itself.

His two lieutenants, thick-set men who had confused violence for purpose, fared little better. Eighteen years each for the kidnapping of Alfie Giles, for dumping what was left of him in the dirt like spoiled meat, and for the drugs that had soaked every part of their lives.

Five lesser faces, now paling under the court's fluorescent glare, were handed five-year stretches and shuffled away, their futures as narrow as the corridors waiting to swallow them.

But in all the pages of evidence, in all the solemn exchanges between counsel, not a breath was drawn about Overlords MC Wales. They were ghosts in the narrative, untouchable, unseen, and scrupulously uninvolved.

Instead, they stepped into the light with a generous donation to the Wales Air Ambulance Charity. A fat cheque, a photo op, a handshake. Praise poured in. Headlines glowed. And the club smiled its quiet, private smile, the kind men wear when the world has looked them square in the face and seen exactly what they wanted it to see.

For Mick, there would be praise, commendations, his story would be sanitised and recounted at the Annual Undercover Conference at Wakefield, where colleagues would mostly shrug nonchalantly and believe that they could have fared just as well. You need that sort of self-belief in that game.

But Mick wasn't there. He was trying to rebuild the pieces of his private life.

6

SHAMROCK

Mick eased the key into the lock of his Knowle apartment as though the slightest scrape might bring the whole bloody world down on him. Gone midnight. He paused, hand on the stiff old Yale, letting the world settle around him. The three-hour wait in that tiny pub outside Cardiff still clung to him like cigarette smoke.

He'd sat there alone, nursing a pint he didn't want, watching the fruit machine cycle through its routine. How long would he have to endure this boredom. The job was done, inevitably, irreversibly, but the nerves still hadn't caught up. Undercover work had a way of hollowing you out that training courses never mentioned.

When Rhys finally shuffled through the pub door, the poor bastard looked like he'd aged a decade on the drive over. He scanned the room with the jumpiness of a man who suddenly knew how many ways things can go wrong. He caught Mick's eye, gave the small, traditional gesture, "want another?", but Mick shook his head. No more waiting. No more anything.

Rhys bought himself a half pint anyway and slid into the seat opposite, shoulders hunched as though the very air might be listening. His voice was a whisper, the sort men use in confessionals.

He told Mick everything, what they'd found at the farm, the whole pantomime, the money stacked like bricks, the clothes half-burnt, halfbloody, the realisation that the rumours about Alfie Giles seemed to be likely. And threaded through all that was Rhys's disbelief, should he admit his disbelief?, that Mick had delivered this. That he'd walked into an impossible game and walked back out with names, evidence, bodies.

"There'll be commendations," Rhys murmured, eyes darting. "From the highest level. Everyone will... well... those who need to know, will hear about this."

The words hit Mick like a slap. Those who need to know. That was the truth of it: he'd disappear again into normality, into what most people would call normality anyway. Rhys's apologies tumbled after; work to do, statements, briefings, more forms than justice ever needed...then he was gone, leaving Mick alone at the table, the fruit machine warbling one last hollow victory tune.

John Wall was waiting at Severn View Services, exactly as planned, a silhouette in the emerging neon glow of the car park. There were men with him, quiet, efficient sorts who handled loose ends and didn't ask what they didn't need to.

They took Mick's bike, his documents, the last physical threads tying Virus to the living world. It should have taken fifteen minutes. It took an hour. Maybe longer. Noir time stretches when you're washing blood off the edges of an alias.

By the time he finally rode away, the bridge behind him was swallowed in darkness.

Tomorrow, the Overlords MC would hear that Virus had met an untimely end on some anonymous stretch of road. They'd mourn him, in their way. Hang his colours on a clubhouse wall and toast the ghost of a man who never really existed. A man who Mick had metaphorically buried in a shallow grave in Cardiff.

***

Bernie wasn't asleep. She hadn't slept properly in months. Mick knew before he crossed the threshold that no warm welcome waited for him.

"What the fuck are you doing here?" Her voice wasn't raised, but it carried the weight of every silence, every missed call, every empty side of the bed.

"I live here, Bern. This is our flat. Our family home."

"Is it? Funny that, I thought a family home needed a family in it. You've been off playing your silly little games while I've been raising two kids who think their dad's a rumour. You missed Emma being born. You missed Danny being born. Christ, I'm surprised you were even here for his conception."

Each word landed like a hammer on wet earth. No drama. No tears. Just the dull thud of truth.

"They Don't know you, Mick. Emma keeps asking when Daddy's coming home. You've no idea what that does to me. So here you are, two years late for your son's birthday, three years late for your daughter's life, and you turn up with gifts like some long-lost uncle." She nodded toward the sofa, a temporary bed for a temporary man.

"I'm going to sleep. I doubt you've forgotten how to kip on your own."

Gifts? Second birthday? Christ. He'd been too deep undercover to keep track of his own blood. They both cried that night.

He slept like a man unshackled. She didn't sleep at all.

Morning cracked open with the shrill, delighted cry of, "Daddy! Daddy!"

Emma barrelled into the room, all red hair and green eyes, the same eyes that had once made him fall in love with her mother. Cuddles, laughs and for Mick, a few regrets.

The unmistakable smell of bacon drifted in from the kitchen diner.

"Come on, you two—breakfast's ready."

Bernie was calmer now, friendlier, and gorgeous. She served him a full fry-up, poured his Yorkshire tea, and even managed a small smile at him, as she winked at Emma.

Danny, perched in his high chair, stared at Mick as if he were a circus act. Tiny fists gripping crustless toast, untouched. The boy's eyes lingered on the tattoos, the graphical records of lies and loyalties that Mick wasn't proud of.

"Yes, he's looking just like his daddy," Bernie said softly, leaning close enough for only Mick to hear the sting that followed, "Poor soul."

She mocked him, but her eyes, normally playful at such times, sold a different message. Resignation. The look a nurse gives a patient that she knows won't make it. There was fondness in her, yes. History, too. But love? That had slipped away somewhere between the missed birthdays and the quiet nights alone. You could only break a heart so many times before it learned to barricade itself. What she felt now was something colder.

And in the hush that followed, Mick knew, there was no undercover job, no commendation, no medal in the world that could fix what he'd let slip through his fingers.

After breakfast, some polite conversation, the scantest details of what Mick had been up to. She really wasn't interested. That boat had sailed long ago. She talked about her family, their concerns for her and their honest opinions about him. He didn't deserve her. They were right.

Then a knock on the door. Sheena, a kindly neighbour had arrived to look after the kids for an hour or so.

"I thought we could go for a stroll over the park and have a chat without any distractions. There's a lot that I need to talk to you about." Bernie sounded as though she had rehearsed that line several times before delivering it.

They took the long path through Knowle Park, the grass still slick from the night's rain, the clouds hanging ominously low. Mick walked half a step behind Bernie, listening without interrupting, calm words that had been expected, but that still landed heavily.

A little while earlier her wedding rings had caught his eye as she had served his breakfast. He noticed they were tighter than he remembered. Flesh had grown around their absence. His absence. A small thing, but the small things tell the truth better than any confession.

Back at the flat he'd seen the flowers, roses, arranged too neatly, too deliberately. The little card that should have been tucked among the stems was gone, torn out like a page that might incriminate. Roses. She'd always said they were a cliché. So whoever sent them didn't know her well but was trying. And trying meant hope. And hope meant someone else had already begun to step into the hollow he'd left.

He let the thought cut him. He deserved the pain. Because no one had forced him down that road. No unseen hand had pushed him into the leather colours, the grime, the lies. No senior had stood over him with a threat. He'd chosen it. Every mile. Every night away.

Every look in the mirror that wasn't sure who it belonged to. And now he was walking beside a woman who had stopped waiting for him a long time ago.

Bernie spoke quietly, her voice soft but with the kind of softness that lives on the far side of exhaustion. She laid out the truth he already knew, the late nights, the empty bed, the newborn he hadn't held, the birthdays he'd missed, the promises that had blown away like cigarette ash. She didn't raise her voice. She didn't need to. The calm made it worse.

As she talked, the rest of the picture filled in like an emerging painting with numbers scene. The maternity ward in Birmingham. Her lying there with their son, waiting for a man wrapped up in someone else's life. And in walks Dr Roger O'Donnell, crisp white coat, easy smile, everything Mick had once been before the job took him. A few gentle words between old colleagues. Months later, a phone call. A coffee. A dinner date. A night where he'd had one drink too many and she'd offered the couch. A decent man inching into the space Mick had abandoned, step by slow step.

A slow burner, she said. She liked him. Dependable. Kind. The sort who turned up when he said he would. The sort a woman could trust not to vanish into smoke. Then that affection had developed into something stronger. She had fallen slowly, certainly, and initially reluctantly, deeply in love.

Mick didn't need to ask for details. The inevitability of it all was as clear as the drizzle settling on the park benches. She needed love. Needed to be seen. Needed to be wanted. To be held. And he'd traded all of that for what exactly? Hard to explain. His choices may have been utterly ridiculous, but they were inevitable.

He looked at her then, really looked. The woman he'd loved before the job hollowed him out. She wasn't angry anymore. And there was no love for him. What sat in her eyes was worse: pity. And pity, Mick knew, is what you feel for someone who can't be saved.

BY THE FIRST OF JULY, 1995, Mick found himself back in the Single Men's Quarters at Digbeth. A convenient, but not entirely suitable, temporary measure. Room 35 wasn't the same room he'd had years ago, but it might as well have been—same peeling paint, same humming radiator, same wardrobe door hanging off its hinge like it had given up asking to be fixed and to the other lads, he was just the stranger in the corridor.

"Have you clocked the old bloke in 35?"

"Yeah. Christ knows who he is, doesn't look like any of ours." The usual script. Young coppers with swagger but no mileage.

Work had gifted him leave—months of untaken days had accrued like dust in a forgotten ledger. Compassionate leave on top of that, if he fancied it. In the end they bundled it all together and told him to disappear until September. Plenty of time to "decompress," which seemed like an appropriate term after being 'under' for so long.

Bernie, for her part, was grateful. First time in years Mick had stepped up properly; turned up for the kids, remembered birthdays, asked after school and colds and nightmares.

It wasn't some pathetic stab at winning her back either; those days had faded long ago. He just wanted things to stop hurting. When he asked to meet Roger, "Doc Rog", as he'd started calling him with a lopsided grin, Bernie had hesitated, but only for a moment.

The doctor was wary, naturally. Men in love tend to be when ghosts from a partner's past come knocking. But he showed up. And Mick respected that.

They met in the quiet corner of a café near the hospital. Roger had the kind of face that tried to look calm but couldn't quite hide the nerves. Mick, tattooed forearms crossed on the table, spoke low, steady, almost gentle.

"I'm glad she found you," he'd said, "Glad she found someone who sees her... really sees her. Someone who can give Emma and Danny what I never managed to." A pause, then the truth, "I never wanted to hurt Bernie. God knows that. I hope someday she can believe it."

Roger had nodded. The sort of nod a man gives when he recognises sincerity in another bloke, even if he doesn't fully understand the world it came from.

In time, Bernie would marry him, her steadfast doctor with the kind eyes—and they would move to Dublin when he took up a pediatrics post at CHI Crumlin. A fresh start across the water, where the air was clean and the political troubles far enough away not to be a threat.

She never chased Mick for money, not once. And he never stopped offering. But she didn't want anything from him except the thing he'd always struggled to give: a stable place in the children's lives.

She told him it wasn't a clean break and that they'd stay in touch. That Emma and Danny would always know they had a father. But life has its own way of cutting ties. And in the end, no matter how gently it happened, a clean break is exactly what they got.

Mick found a scrap of skin on his arm the ink hadn't already claimed and offered it up to the needle. A shamrock this time, three leaves, three initials: B. E. D. And underneath a name. "Nancy". A poor man's shrine to a life he'd fumbled.

Now and again, catching his reflection in a train window or the smeared glass of some city doorway, the green flash of it would wink back at him. A reminder. A reproach. And for a fleeting second, a heartbeat, no more, the hard man's eyes would glaze, the world smudging at the edges.

Then it would pass, as all things did, leaving him alone again with the ink, the ghosts, and the quiet he'd earned.

7

ANOTHER DANCE OR TWO

Whether "the brass" appreciated him or not, and many of them didn't , Mick Dorrington's successes had reflected better on them than they deserved.

They too easily muttered predictable things behind closed office doors: loose cannon, maverick, law unto himself. Words the timid used when faced with a man who went where they wouldn't dare.

Even so, none of them were daft enough to send him back in uniform, despite their illconsidered assessment that a spell pounding the streets would do him good. Not after everything he'd done. He still had his uses.

His future lay elsewhere now, new names, new backstories, new ghosts waiting to be stitched to his shoulders. The outlaw biker world was closed to him for good; a burned bridge left smouldering in the past. Common sense, really. You don't stroll back into a den after helping sack it. There were other dark corners to disappear into. Other circuits where a man like Mick could be useful.

When Bernie finally left the flat in Knowle, their flat he'd once kidded himself, and stepped into a gentler life as Mrs. O'Donnell, wife to a polished pediatrician, a good man, a reliable man, with soft hands and no secrets, it was as though a door shut quietly behind

Mick. No slam, no tantrum. Just the quiet click of inevitability. She took their two beautiful children to Dublin, a city where they would have a happier, more settled future, while Mick packed what little was really his and walked away without looking back. No point in looking back. Too late for regrets.

He couldn't stay in Single Men's Quarters for long. Too cramped. Too many young coppers with loud voices and empty lives gawping at 'the old bloke in Room 35'. He wasn't old of course —but undercover work ages a man from the inside out.

He caught his reflection once, in a panel of polished metal in the corridor, and saw someone who'd lived more than his years. Someone he barely recognised.

So, he signed the papers for a small rented flat in central Birmingham's canal side. The city's sons and daughters liked to boast it had more waterways than Venice, a strange kind of pride. In truth, the canals were relics from another age: the lifelines of the Industrial Revolution, left to stagnate for far too long, but enough space for developers to create shiny trendy residential zones that attracted single thirty-somethings, yuppies and young professionals.

Despite not really identifying with that demographic, it suited him.

The nights there were quiet and peaceful. On some evenings, he would stroll along the old tow paths, just yards from the bustling streets of the city centre, the city lights mirrored on the canal's surface, and the world seemed almost tolerable. Occasionally, Mick would notice himself caressing the skin where his most recent tattoo had been carefully carved. A shamrock. It no longer hurt.

As time inevitably rolled on, days blending into weeks, weeks into months, Mick eased himself back into the old rhythms. There was a comfort to it, of sorts: the slow churn of legend-building when he wasn't buried in the mechanics of an undercover job, the long hours in the dim hush of a surveillance car when there was nothing else to do. Familiar, predictable, almost soothing in its own hollow way.

He made a point of taking on support roles for other U/Cs whenever he could. Partly to shake off the lingering notion held by some that he was a prima donna who lived only for centre stage; partly because he recognised how much there always was to learn by simply watching others work.

His track record might have looked impressive on paper, but he knew better than most that feeling invincible was the first step towards making a fatal mistake. There were always lessons waiting, and the trick was to pick them up before they were taught the hard way.

Every now and then a substantial result would come along, something that broke through the monotony. Seizures of forged banknotes and traveler's cheques with daunting face values, stacks of paper that could look like millions or nothing at all depending on who was holding them.

A job in Germany, an amphetamine factory had been offered to him purely off the back of Carousel, a reminder that his name still travelled further than he ever intended it to.

Meetings with Dutch traffickers in Amsterdam to support an operation in Scotland, multi-kilo cannabis hauls, the strange déjà vu of finding himself once again waiting at a familiar motorway service station for some unlucky courier to arrive with whatever illicit cargo he'd arranged to 'buy' or had been asked to 'test'.

Conversations with operational targets had begun to feel like scenes,from a play that had been staged far too many times. The lines were always the same, the same forced bravado, the same cautious probing, the same predictable pauses while someone pretended to think. It was a familiar dance that looked like negotiation from the outside, but Mick knew better. There was never any real give-and-take, never any mystery to it. One person set the pace and called the tune, even if the other poor soul hadn't worked that out yet. It was choreography, pure and simple. And that was the problem. The predictability of it all. The sameness.

What had once quickened his blood now merely tugged at the edges of his patience. He could feel the stories blurring together, one deal here, another meeting there, every face starting to look like a faint echo of the last. Even the adrenaline had lost its sharpness, like a blade dulled from years of overuse. The work still mattered, of course it did, but there was a quiet exhaustion beneath the surface now, something he couldn't ignore. A sense that while the job kept moving forward, some part of him was slowly being left behind.

The commendations continued to arrive, quietly, steadily, as they always had. And he accepted them the same way he approached everything now , with a tired nod, a polite thank you, and a feeling that each one weighed just a touch heavier than the last.

The work was still the work, but something in him was beginning to fray at the edges. The pace felt the same; he was the one slowing. The days stretched on, and he kept moving through them, but the effort of doing so was no longer something he could easily ignore.

By the summer of 1998, the strain had begun to show. Mick surprised even himself when he announced that he needed a proper break, a few weeks away somewhere warm, where the days drifted by without a single thought of work. His colleagues had been delighted, some joked that he'd finally joined the rest of them in being human, but privately he knew the truth went deeper.

He was tired, bone-deep tired in a way that no early night or quiet weekend could mend. For the first time, he allowed himself to recognise it: the edges of his once-boundless enthusiasm had started to fray, and the job, his job, was beginning to wear him down. It was a new experience.

He told himself that what he needed was one of those "trial separations" that jaded couples sometimes talked about, the sort that gave breathing space and perspective. Not an ending, but a pause. Time to work on the things he'd let slide, his patience, his energy, maybe even that fierce dedication he used to take such pride in.

With a bit of distance, he hoped, he might rediscover the appetite for a life he had once loved without question. He didn't expect miracles. Just a reset. A chance to feel steady again. And, if he was lucky, it wouldn't take very long.

It was as good a moment as any for Mick to step back. The Regional Crime Squads, had, by then, been emerged in controversies about their methods and concerns about corruption, and had been dissolved that April, their officers folded, at least in theory, into the freshly minted National Crime Squad (NCS).

For many RCS officers, the uncertainty of re-badged roles and new structures had bred a quiet unease, the sort that seeped into conversations over plastic mugs of tea and lingered long after shift's end.

Mick had felt the strain more keenly than most, the accumulative weight of years spent slipping into other lives pressing harder than he cared to admit. With the future in flux and the walls of the job seeming to close in a little each day, even he had to concede that he needed a holiday, needed space, sun, and silence, before the frayed edges of his nerves gave way entirely.

But where to go? Greece crossed his mind first, but he wasn't sure he wanted to face memories of that brief, hopeful honeymoon—days that felt like someone else's life now.

Spain was another possibility, but too many faces from too many case files had drifted out there to start new 'lives'. He could practically see himself running into one of them in a restaurant in Marbella, or Estepona, or anywhere on the 'Costa del Crime'.

The Canaries, though—they had a pleasant, distant ring to them. He'd heard they were peaceful, easy-going, somewhere you could simply exist for a while without being on edge. A quiet holiday in the sun.

A bit of research and he concluded that what he specifically needed was a fortnight's 'all inclusive' at the Hotel Grande Teneriffe, in Costa Adeje, Teneriffe.

A quick trip to the travel agency and the holiday was booked. A bit extravagant, but he could easily spend two weeks doing exactly what he wanted to do, without actually stepping outside of the modern complex. That appealed to him.

He didn't want to party, or sight see, or buy souvenirs, or get involved in any holiday romance or even casual sexual activity. Sun loungers, cocktails, his 'Walkman', and the company of a good book was all he needed. And the luxury of being isolated with his own thoughts, therapeutic meditation without any mantric humming.

In no time at all he was sitting on a British Airways Boeing 737 taxiing down the runway at Birmingham Airport heading for a welldeserved break.

He had chosen well. Within days he eased into a gentle rhythm, a sort of soft holiday cadence that asked little of him. He was up before breakfast most mornings, slipping into one of the hotel's three pools for twenty unhurried minutes of steady, almost meditative swimming.

Afterwards he would let the warm, not fierce, early morning air dry him before wandering back to his room. Shorts, a T-shirt, and flip-flops, and then on to the buffet for something light.

The rest of the day unfolded in what became predictable famil-iarity: sun-lounger, music through cheap headphones, the occasional chapter of a book, and, during those first few days at least, an attempt at honest self-examination.

That part mattered. The honest self-analysis. Sometimes awkward, sometimes bleak, occasionally surprising. If he was ever going to move forward in any meaningful way, he first had to look over his shoulder.

Only by facing his own long shadow could he hope to reclaim his narrative, sorting through the muddle of strengths, shortfalls, and the shifting boundaries of the man he had become. By stripping the thoughts back and examining them carefully, forensically, he hoped to find a little clarity. A sense of direction. Something steady enough to build on.

And inevitably, he found himself comparing two versions of himself: the young constable standing outside the central station in Birmingham, blue serge immaculate, proud, but with a few nerves tingling with hope and anticipation... and the man who now lay beneath a Spanish sun, still capable and still respected, but carrying compromises he rarely admitted to.

The undercover names, Micky Dee, Micky Robinson, and the rest of that revolving cast, had made choices Mick Dorrington would never have imagined himself making. He had always told himself that those choices weren't his. They belonged to someone else. A mask. A persona. A necessary alias. But however noble the intention, he could see now that it was still a fiction.

Then there was the matter of his ego. He had always pretended he didn't need praise, batting away compliments with the same easy shrug he offered as a young man treading the boards as Richard III, soaking in the applause of his teachers and his bewildered audience, but claiming he didn't care for it. Praise had fueled him then; in truth, it still did. How many times had he heard it?

"I could never do what you do, Mick."

"Of course you could". He would say.

But he had always known they probably couldn't. And he had always known that part of him enjoyed that fact.

In the steady, unforgiving Spanish sunlight, Mick found himself reaching a conclusion he had never expected to form with such clarity. He didn't much like Mick Dorrington. Not as he was now.

And that confession, quiet and unadorned, made him feel tired and weary, like the words of the anthem adopted by his favoured football team. He had actually reached the end of the road.

AS THE INCOMING 737 touched down on the tarmac at BHX, it wasn't quite the same Mick Dorrington who'd boarded the outbound flight a few weeks earlier. This one stepped off the aircraft a couple of pounds heavier, skin tanned to the colour of burnished copper, shoulder-length hair bleached to a lazy blond by the island sun. He looked younger, or at least less burdened than the man who'd slipped away for a break that was even more needed than he had realised.

His taxi wouldn't be outside yet. It never was. He'd half expected the usual nod from Customs, the inevitable hand on the elbow. He'd always played along, never pulling rank, never mentioning what he really was. It all made good material for the next time he needed to spin a yarn, anyway. He dragged his battered Samsonite off the carousel and steered it towards the green channel. He caught the two uniforms before they caught him—if they were even trying. They stood in that way uniforms do when they 're pretending not to watch someone. Their eyes brushed past him, lingered a fraction too long, then moved on.

For once there was no raised hand, no gentle, 'Excuse me, sir'. He walked straight through. A small thing, but it felt like a quiet confirmation that whatever had shifted inside him out there in the sundrenched days and quiet nights... it had stayed shifted.

The new Mick Dorrington was home. A couple of days getting used to the cooler days, at least not Tenerife temperatures anyway, maybe slipping out for a coffee or beer in town and showing off his healthy tan to anyone who happened to notice, and then it would be back to work.

He had no idea what his future would hold. He knew that the decision he was about to convey would be greeted by his seniors with, first disbelief, then disappointment, then relief, both for themselves and for him.

He had decided it was time to move on

8

MOVING ON

Unusually, Mick parked his grey BMW M3 on the car park adjacent to the station entrance in Bourneville Lane. He'd normally park some distance away in case prying eyes were trying to identify vehicles that belonged to police officers. And as unlikely as that was, that was just the way his mind had worked. Not anymore. So, the Beemer was left in plain sight. He didn't care.

Sporting a fresh, modern trim, some length on top, casually brushed back but naturally falling into bangs, resting on the top of the ears at the sides, just reaching the collar at the back, and a much shorter, neater goatee, a young uniformed police woman, who Mick had briefly flirted with in the canteen, had to give him a second look to be certain it was him.

Mick noticed her reaction and smiled.

Through a window, he spotted Jonas Peters sitting in the canteen. He was in deep conversation with a smart suited man who Mick didn't recognise, but the glare of light on the windowpane diffused the scene. DI Peters had also spotted Mick, a word mouthed, and almost immediately the suit turned his head to look towards Mick.

"Hope he's not going to be long. We need to crack on," Mick muttered to himself.

On his way into the office, the returning prodigal was greeted with the usual racket: a couple of the NCS lads offered wolf whistles from across the car park, and the former Drugs Wing detectives already waiting in his office broke into predictable laughter at his newly sun-bleached hair and holiday tan.

DS Dan Cooper whose call name was 'Bomb-scare' on the radio comms, asked if Mick had been moonlighting in the adult film trade and suggested they start calling him 'Porn Star', a line that earned the expected chuckles but also reminded Mick how quickly such throw-away nicknames tended to stick, as 'Yoghurt' had discovered. She had spent weeks thinking her handle came from the time she'd spilt yoghurt down herself when the surveillance car had lurched into a sudden takeover, only for Mick to later learn from the others, with a wince, that it really referred to her being "thick and fruity".

The banter washed over him in the familiar way it always had, but underneath it all he felt the slight sag of fatigue, as though the jokes belonged to a world he was stepping back into out of habit rather than desire.

One of his closest allies on the unit was 'Bambi', DC Steve Cooper. He'd earned the nickname after slipping on ice during a foot surveillance and quite literally sliding into the target. Once or twice he'd helped to support Mick on an undercover operation, by turning up as his brother. When they first met, people had been amazed by how physically similar they were. There were jokes about them being separated at birth. Pretty much straight away they always referred to each other as 'Bro'.

"Yo, Bro!" Steve shouted,"Hope you've bought something nice back".

"Yeah Bro, but a couple of shots of penicillin should get rid of it."

Inane office banter often kept spirits up when things weren't going well.

Mick dropped four oversized bags of Lacasitos and Conguitos and a box of Huevositos onto the biscuit table, every police office had one of those, his token offerings from Tenerife. They'd linger for a bit before most of them inevitably found their way into the bin, but it was the gesture that mattered. The bottle of Porthos Vodka he'd picked up would stay sealed until the next leaving do; with any luck he wouldn't have too long a wait.

He noticed Dan Cooper fielding a phone call he clearly hadn't wanted to answer, short, clipped responses, then the receiver slammed down.

"Eh Mick, the Magistrate's after you."

Everyone had their own nickname, even the ones who rarely went near surveillance; DI Jonas Peters was 'Magistrate' thanks to his initials, JP— Justice of the Peace.

Mick half-smiled to himself: probably a welfare check. How was the break? Feeling refreshed? You're looking well. The usual ritual some bosses stuck to out of obligation, but Jonas wasn't one of those.

He was one of the rare few who genuinely cared, which somehow made the whole thing feel heavier rather than lighter. At least Mick would now get the chance to deliver the speech that he had rehearsed too many times already.

His sharp knock on the DI's unusually closed door - he always kept it slightly ajar to stay in touch with the office banter, and to keep an eye on comings and goings - and Mick was summoned to enter.

Jonas wasn't at his desk, instead he was sitting on one of the chairs that surrounded his coffee table, the place where welfare chats or informal meetings are conducted. Next to him was the chap that Mick had seen with Jonas in the canteen. A senior was Mick's soon to be confirmed assessment. A pot of fresh tea had been made and poured.

"Mick, I would like you to meet Detective Superintendent McAllister from Merseyside Police."

"It's Jock, Jock McAllister. Nice to finally meet you Mick."

A gentle Scottish lilt. Edinburgh maybe? Mick shook his extended hand firmly.

"Take a seat Mick. By the way, please call me Jock. Like I say, it is really good to meet you at last. I wanted to get your opinion on a problem that I've been struggling with for some time now. It's causing me sleepless nights, and I certainly need my beauty sleep."

Mick smiled politely. Yes, Edinburgh, but also a brushing of Scouse was detectable.

"Tell me, Mick, have you ever heard of the name Victor Harland?"

'Call me Jock' had asked the question with the sort of knowing smile that told Mick the answer hardly mattered; it was a formality, a box to tick. There wasn't a copper in the country with even a passing link to drugs work who didn't know the name Victor Harland, drug lord, racketeer, bully-boy emperor of the Liverpool backstreets, untouchable' being the word most often hissed in station corridors.

Jock knew full well that Mick would have heard the tales during those long, half-forgotten years when he was living under borrowed names and borrowed loyalties; stories traded in smoke-filled bars and grimy cafés, each one adding another layer to the myth of a man no one could quite reach. And now, after everything, it seemed the inevitable wheel had turned. Harland's shadow had finally stretched into Mick's world, whether he liked it or not.

The briefing that Jock delivered was detailed to the point of being almost forensic. He laid out Harland's life story, along with the histories of anyone who had ever drifted near his organisation, dissecting them with a precision that made it obvious this wasn't just work; Harland was Jock's obsession.

He'd weighed every investigative avenue, carefully listing the strengths and weaknesses of each, only to reach the same conclusion every time. Even after meeting with the Head of the Met's SO10 Undercover Policing Unit, the verdict had been unavoidable: the operation simply wasn't ready. There were no access agents, no exploitable weaknesses, no cracks to prise open. And a long-term infiltration, already a perilous undertaking, would be near impossible without constant close protection, which would in turn cripple any chance of success.

Mick had asked questions at various opportune moments - had this, that, or the other been considered; they always had, and Jock was able to say why they had then been discounted as options. In truth, Mick had only asked to be polite, to show willing, to take an interest. When Jock had finally finished talking, his eyes looked at Mick in a way that begged for some optimism.

"I'm out of options. I know that you have a reputation for being able to think outside of the box. I've had the Carousel briefing. Very impressive. Thought I would get your thoughts."

There was a short, thoughtful pause before Mick offered his summary with quiet finality: SO10 had been right, some jobs belonged in the 'Too Hard To Do' tray, and attempting an infiltration would be suicidal, especially in a world where Harland had already bought influence in the police. He had no other suggestions.

Jonas Peters listened with a quiet pride; Jock with the defeated acceptance of a man hearing confirmation of his expected fear.

Then came Jonas's question that really didn't need to be asked, but that deserved a response; Was there anything Mick wanted to ask the Superintendent?

Mick sat for a moment, the weight of inevitability settling on his shoulders, before he broke the hush with a calm that surprised even himself.

He had walked into the NCS office that morning with a clarity he hadn't felt in years, ready at last to say the words he'd rehearsed endlessly under the Tenerife sun and in the quiet hours: he was retiring from undercover work. Not a sabbatical, not a pause, but a clean and final severing of the cord that had tied him to a life lived through borrowed names and borrowed faces.

The decision hadn't sprung from panic, nor from the gentle nudges of worried friends, nor even from the half-hidden concern in the eyes of those who understood the toll this world exacted. It was simply the outcome of months of cool, deliberate thought, an acceptance that whatever fire had once driven him had dimmed, and that the man he had become could no longer thrive in the shadows where Mick Dorrington's ghosts had learned to live.

Nothing would dissuade him. He didn't much care what the future held. He had pounded the streets once before in a blue serge suit and a heavy helmet, and he could do it again if he had to. Maybe some friendly DI would find space for him in a CID office; maybe there'd be a teaching post going at Tally Ho! or somewhere. Options existed, and sooner or later one of them would open its door.

He was prepared to give Superintendent Jock McAllister his full attention, politeness, if nothing else, demanded that, but none of it was going to change the course he'd already chosen. Nothing in the Detective Superintendent's meticulous briefing, comprehensive though it was, could have shifted Mick's resolve to step away from the life he'd been living. It was a decision made coolly, soberly, without leaning on emotions or the well-meant advice of friends and colleagues. He was done. Finished. Time to move on, wherever that path led.

No, it wasn't what Jock McAllister had said that reached him, it was the way he had said it.

McAllister spoke with a fierce, unembarrassed passion. He laid out every option that had been examined and, correctly, dismissed. Still, he refused to throw in the towel. Even when the logic screamed that the case was dead in the water, Jock pushed on, willing to metaphorically 'flog a dead horse' rather than stand idly by. It was commitment, in its purest form.

And Mick understood that. He understood it far too well.

Jock McAllister had an insurmountable, hopeless problem, and he wanted Mick's opinion on what he might do next.

Despite himself, despite the tiredness that had settled into his bones and the resolve he'd carried through the door that morning, Mick felt something shift.

There was a quiet dignity in Jock's refusal to give up, a stubborn commitment that reminded Mick of the man he'd once hoped to be. It was alluring and it was seductive.

And at that moment, almost before he realised it was happening, Mick felt the familiar pull of duty slip past his defences.

Jock hadn't persuaded him. He hadn't needed to. Mick was simply, and unmistakably, drawn in.

And that is why Mick had asked that final shocking revealing question of Jock McAllister, the question that made DI Jonas Peters choke out the mouthful of tea he'd only just sipped.

"When would you like me to start?"

9

AS YOU WERE

Jock's question, "What do you need me to do now, Mick?" wasn't quite the usual, "How do we go about this?" line he'd heard so many times before. There was something almost deferential in it, something that suggested Jock understood that he was stepping into someone else's world now, not bringing Mick into his.

His answer to Mick's earlier "Do you trust me?" had carried the same tone.

"Do I have any choice?" Honest, unvarnished, and oddly reassuring.

The next steps were never Mick's to sort out. The machinery had to grind into motion, and logistics were Jock's burden. Mick might still have been classed as a national asset, but the National Crime Squad were about to lose him for...well, nobody quite knew how long. One of the senior officers had already made his view plain; he wasn't paying for one of his men to disappear indefinitely. The NCS was still new, still proving itself, and every penny mattered. Their priorities weren't necessarily Mick's though.

So came the miles of road travel, the quiet negotiations in offices that smelled of old carpets and instant coffee, the phone calls that grew wearier each time. Eventually, an agreement was struck. Mick was to be seconded to Merseyside Police for an open-ended period. They would cover his wages, overtime, expenses—and, on paper at least, his wellbeing.

The force's finance officers believed that Michael Dorrington, who they only knew existed on paper, had been engaged as a contractor. They didn't need to know more than that.

Before he left, Mick was called to the office of the NCS Deputy Director. The handshake was firm and formal; the smile...practiced.

"All the very best of luck—or should I say, break a leg?"

The theatrical jibe was meant lightly, but it landed with an ironic weight that the Deputy Director would never fully appreciate.

And then the final line, delivered with the detachment of someone merely completing paperwork.

"You are, of course, aware that there may not be a position for you here when you return... whenever that may be."

Mick nodded, already feeling the familiar heaviness settling across his shoulders. He had heard variations of that message his entire career... nothing is guaranteed, don't expect too much, don't expect anything at all.

Mick didn't expect anything. He wasn't that foolhardy. Still—he was going. Because Jock had asked. Because the job was impossible. And because some small, stubborn part of him could not walk away from an impossible job.

OVER THE COMING months Mick Dorrington disappeared, and Michael David Vaughan, Mikey, was hauled out of cold storage, brushed down, and reanimated for another tour on the dark side.

Mikey had drifted through two or three operations in the northwest. He'd never been one of the headliners, just a reliable money man in decent rags, even a suit sometimes, and a face nobody remembered five minutes later.

A walk-on part with enough swagger to be useful, but not enough to be dangerous. He was on the books for helping lift fifty kilos of cocaine from a lorry rolling towards Manchester, after he'd flashed a clean quarter-million in cash to convince the dealers that he was the money behind the guys they were dealing with.

There had also been the five kilos of China White, (3-methyl fentanyl), that were pulled from a car 'randomly' stopped on the M6 near Sandbach. The load had been destined for Mikey, of course. He eventually received a groveling message about the unfortunate interception of his parcel, all apologies and promises to make it right. Mikey had told them they were amateurs and that they could stick the whole thing where the sun didn't shine.

He'd also become known in some of the boozers in Crewe, Sandbach and Warrington. To help build up the legend, he was given the cash to buy gold and sometimes secondhand jewelry at cost price from a friendly source in Birmingham's Jewelry Quarter. He could then hawk that out at a significant financial loss around the pubs and clubs of wherever he was trying to establish a reputation. He would make a point of insisting that none of his goods were 'hot', and that was the truth. But no-one believed him. It was a cost-effective method of buying the reputation he was developing.

One of his customers, a licensee in Warrington, was overheard bragging to a local that he had known Mikey for years, they'd practically grown up together. Funny how people liked to do that. Pretend that they knew him more than they really did. Harmless, unless later there was a hunting party looking for Mikey who would learn of the boast.

So, Mikey Vaughan had a past, threadbare, a little ugly around the edges, but convincing enough. And none of it had ever stirred suspicion.

Mikey Vaughan was the foundation on which Mick would build a character who would hopefully attract, meet, befriend, earn the trust of, and eventually bring down, Victor Harland. That was the plan.

They just hadn't met yet.

~

BY THE SPRING OF "99, Mikey had settled himself into a modern duplex perched along the Manchester Ship Canal, in Warrington , a slick little place with enough glass and steel to feel new, but still close enough to the water to give him that steadying hum of familiarity. He spent a few weeks making the place his own, while easing into the role the way a man slips into a forgotten jacket that he'd rediscovered at the back of his wardrobe. Then he began drifting back into the orbit of those who already "knew" him. A few careful conversations with the right faces, a shrug about 'a bit of bother back in the Midlands', nothing specific, nothing that needed spelling out.

In their world, silence filled in the details far better than words could. By the end of the week the whispers had done their job: Mikey Vaughan, Brummie lad, bit tasty, allegedly on the run from Birmingham's finest. A decent bloke though. Straight enough. Worth buying a pint for.

Within a couple of months there were two, maybe three pubs and a couple of eating houses in Warrington where Mikey never had to reach for his wallet. His benefactors were easy to spot, thick new gold chains hanging on necks that hadn't earned them, wives or girlfriends, sometimes both, flashing matching sets, courtesy of that guy from 'Birminum' amazing how many people mis-pronounced the name of the UKs second largest city. It wasn't victory. Not even close. But it was a foothold. A platform. And now, the next step could begin.

The steady flow of expense claims, handed in via a trusted Manchester-based U/C who Mikey had worked with a couple of times, told Jock McAllister that Mikey's journey had begun.

SOMETIMES THE JOB came down to pure blind luck. You could plan yourself into a coma, play every angle, grease every palm, and still end up flat on your back if fortune didn't fancy you that day.

Mick had always said there were only two kinds of coppers, those who were good, and those who were lucky. Same applied to undercover work, though he'd learned the hard way that the line between the two was paper-thin.

Most people wrote it off as his way of dodging praise, but he knew better. He'd won the game more than once because the universe had rolled the dice in his favour, not because he was some kind of genius. And now, staring down the impossible road ahead, he could only hope that luck still remembered his name.

Over the months, Mick—Mikey—started occasionally drifting into Liverpool's nightlife. Clubs like Cream, 051, and The Grafton were worlds apart from the biker bars and rock-festival mud he was used to. Too bright, too loud, too desperate. But needs must. He did what felt natural to him. A quiet corner, a half-ignored drink, and that battered Nokia 3210 permanently pressed to his ear as if he were conducting business no one else needed to overhear. Bit by bit, the picture sharpened. He started to look like the kind of bloke who could get you what you wanted...if the price was right and the trust was earned.

"Got any Charlie?" became the soundtrack to his nights. He'd shrug, shake his head.

"No, mate, not into it," letting the line hang just long enough for someone watching to wonder. And then, with the faintest flick of the hand, he'd pass a wrap to a 'stranger', one of the new kids from the undercover pool, eager to cut their teeth and grateful for the chance. A performance for an audience he'd never meet.

Every so often, a whisper floated back to Jock; some detective in the Merseyside Drug Squad claiming a source had mentioned a new Brummie sniffing around town, maybe shifting coke, maybe something bigger. Not enough to pull him in, not yet. Just enough to keep Mikey Vaughan's name warm in the right rumour mills.

Jock tucked the intel away. Maybe, when the time was right, they'd let one of the more seasoned local faces spot Mikey in the cells. Let the story build the way good stories always do, slowly, quietly, until it's the only version people believe.

Luck. Timing. Whispered lies. All the usual tools, and Mick knew he'd need every last one of them. The job ahead was still huge, still impossible—but the city was gradually starting to notice he existed.

That was the small victory.

New Years Eve. Was the world going to grind to a halt as the Millennium Bug hit? No one knew.

The newspapers had been full of it. No one in Liverpool seemed worried. Partly to stay in cover, and partly because it would be good to have a night of fun, Mikey was one of about 250,000 who attended the Millennium Party hosted by Cream at the Pier Head.

Even if he hadn't been working, this was a good way to welcome in a new century. Lasers and projections illuminated the Three Graces, (the Royal Liver Building, the Cunard Building, and the Port of Liverpool Building), while Fatboy Slim, Pete Tong, Orbital, Paul Oakenfold, Darren Emerson, and the Stereophonics took their turns to entertain the raucous crowd while a red LED clock was counting out the dying embers of the 20th Century.

Mikey had drifted down to the Pier Head earlier than most some-time around eight, the sky still nursing the last bruises of dusk. He grabbed a burger from a stall that smelled of onions, sea-spray and cheap fryer oil, Scouse cuisine at its purest. Someone, he never did clock who, pressed a plastic cup of wine into his hand with the easy generosity of festival nights and strangers who think they've made a friend.

He lifted the drink in a quiet, private toast. To Bernie. To Emma and Danny. And to Doc Rog, a good man, better future. No tremor in his hand, no sting behind the eyes. Those tears had been spent long ago. Then he found himself a spot with a clean line of sight to the stage and the crowd swelling around it.

He let the night wash over him, the bass thrum, the neon spill, the sweat-soaked joy of people who believed that next year was going to be better than the last one had been. House music wasn't his bag; not really. His soul leaned more towards distorted guitars and the thump of a kick drum played by someone with calloused fingers. But months spent walking Liverpool's nightscape, trying to belong, had taught him to hear the pulse behind the noise.

And so he stood there—anonymous but alert—sipping warm wine from a flimsy plastic cup while the headline DJs shook the river air.

Then, she landed on his foot like a dropped feather, an attractive brunette with luminous eyes and a warm, mixed-heritage complexion that caught every stray glimmer of light.

"Oooh, sorry love. Sorry." Definitely local. Definitely gorgeous.

He'd had half a dozen toes trodden on that evening; she was the only one who apologised. She drifted back towards the couple she'd arrived with, then hesitated, turned, and laid a gentle hand on his arm.

"I do know you, don't I? Where do I know you from?"

He'd rehearsed lines for this very moment— every U/C had. "I'm certain if I'd met you before, I'd remember."

A smile, soft. A wink, friendly rather than forward.

"You're not from Liverpool. Let me guess... Buurmmingum." She delivered the accent with an exaggerated flourish and a warm giggle.

"I'll have you know I don't have a regional accent," he replied in his best BBC voice, "But yes—Buurmmingum."

She tilted her head, "So...what's a girl got to do to get offered a drink around here?"

Mikey took the hint. A few quiet words to her companions; a hug for the girl, a half-hearted nod from the bloke; and the pair wandered off, leaving space for something new to unfold. Over a couple of hours and a couple of glasses of wine, he learned more about her than she realised she'd revealed.

Michelle O "Grady. Thirty-one. Single. Divorced. No kids, couldn't have them. Irish grandparents. Liverpool born and bred. Dad from a West Indian family, now deceased, mum a Scouser. Worked in finance. Proud aunt to twin girls, Jane and Jasmine. Sharp mind. Warm laugh. A little lonely.

And she believed she was sharing a bottle with Mikey Vaughan, thirty-five, divorced, a businessman from Birmingham, licking his wounds in the northwest. A man scarred by a cheating wife who kept him from his daughter. Just enough truth to anchor the lie.

It wasn't much, but it was enough. Michelle leaned in. Wanted more. The spark between them was immediate, bright, and dangerous. It would be a long job, a very long job, and Mick felt the old rule cracking, 'never get involved while in character'.

But this felt different. Thrilling. Breath-stealing. Impossible to ignore.

Hand in hand, they eventually strolled back to her sister and brother-in-law. Michelle was grinning; her sister clocked the gesture instantly and offered Mikey an approving smile.

"Mikey, this is my sister, Sarah."

"Great to meet you. Happy New Year." A polite peck on the cheek.

"Hey you, she's spoken for," Michelle teased. "And this is my brother-in-law, Jamie."

"Hello Jamie, Mikey Vaughan." He anticipated that Jamie would reply in similar fashion. It would be wise to know who he was.

A handshake, soft, damp, limp. It told Mick everything he needed to know.

"Hello, Mikey. I'm Jamie Grant. Respect!"

The name immediately resonated. Jamie Grant. He had heard it before. He could hear it pronounced in Jock's soft Scottish lilt. A crowd of a quarter of a million and Mikey had just shaken hands with a man who had once been very close to Victor Harland. It's better to be lucky than good.

IN THE COLD daylight of New Year's Day, 2000, everything snapped into focus with the kind of clarity that only a hangover and a guilty conscience can deliver. The music had stopped, the crowds had vanished, and what remained was the truth he'd been trying not to look at too closely. If Mikey took things further with Michelle, and Christ, he wanted to, he wouldn't just be bending his own rules. He'd be shattering them.

Police undercover doctrine was unambiguous: no emotional entanglements while under. No romantic ties. No sex. No exceptions.

Cross that line and you weren't just reckless, you were a criminal. Procurement by deception. Two years inside.

But the law wasn't the worst of it. What chilled him wasn't the thought of prison; it was the thought of Michelle. She wasn't some forgettable pub flirtation or a disposable alias-night mistake. She was warm, sharp, grounded, the kind of woman who made a man forget he was supposed to be someone else. And that made her dangerous.

Because the job didn't care who she was. The job only cared who her brother-in-law was. Jamie Grant. And Jamie Grant might, just might, be a door. A crack in the wall around Harland. A chance so small it barely existed, but a chance nonetheless. And if Mikey let things run their natural course with Michelle... well, he could all but guarantee the introductions he needed. That was the game laid bare. Simple. Ugly. Tempting.

Mikey felt the pull of it—duty, opportunity, desire—all tangled up in a messy bouquet of barbed wire. He could almost hear Jock's voice, 'Whatever it takes'.

But there were some lines you couldn't step over without leaving pieces of yourself behind. The question was whether Mikey Vaughan still had enough of Mick Dorrington left in him to know the difference.

He sat alone in his flat, the canal outside flat and grey as slate, and realised that sooner or later he'd have to choose the woman... or the mission. And whichever way he leaned, someone was going to get hurt. Probably him.

When Jock got the update a few days later, he didn't pause to blow the steam from his tea. The moment Mick mentioned Michelle, Jamie Grant, and the thin thread that might, just might, lead toward Harland, Jock's eyes hardened into something close to relief. Not joy. Not triumph. Just the grim satisfaction of a man who's finally found the only crack in a fortress he's spent years battering.

He didn't hesitate.

"Then that's the road We're taking," he said, as if the matter were already history. And in a way, it was. Because if someone didn't stop Harland, lives would continue to be lost. Rivals would vanish from street corners. A few unlucky innocents would get caught between bullets meant for other men. Families would shatter. Kids would grow up without a parent. Jock knew it. Mick knew it. And between the two of them hung the unspoken truth; this wasn't a choice. Not really. It was inevitability dressed up as strategy.

If there was even the faintest chance that Mick—Mikey— could use this accidental spark with Michelle to edge closer to Jamie Grant... and from Jamie to Harland... then they both understood the rules had already changed. Lines would blur. There would be a risk to everyone. Reputations could be damaged. Some would be hurt, badly hurt. Possibly irreparably hurt.

But Jock didn't blink.

"If Michelle is the bridge, then she's the bridge you cross. Carefully."

10

THE LONG SLOW DANCE

Michelle only let her little Motorola flip phone trill once before snapping it open, breathless and bright, as though she'd been holding the air in her chest all week.

"Mikey. I thought you'd given me the cold shoulder... that's not why you're calling, is it?"

It wasn't. Not remotely.

He told her he wanted to see her again, nothing heavy, just a coffee, a chat, a bit of daylight instead of the murk they'd met in. He could pick her up somewhere quiet, if that helped.

It helped. More than she let on.

Later, in the café, they sat watching their untouched coffees cool and thicken into that familiar film, the sort people idly stir when they're avoiding saying something real.

Mikey looked into those dark, luminous eyes of hers and let the story spill out. The betrayal, the divorce, the slow unravelling of a man who'd once thought himself indestructible. A performance, yes, but one stitched together from truths that still had teeth.

He told her he wasn't ready. Not properly. Not for the whole thing. He wanted her in his life, that much he couldn't hide, but the wounds were fresh, the ground unsteady. He needed time to get his head straight, and he hoped she'd still be there when he did.

Then came the rest; the legal wrangling over access to a daughter he adored, the ghosts he'd fled from in the Midlands, Warrington chosen for its distance and for the friends who wouldn't ask awkward questions. A few 'minor problems' with the law, he said lightly, nothing she needed to worry about. All done and dusted.

And Michelle believed him. Not because she was naïve, but because he wore the damage well, like it was something he'd earned. Under normal circumstances, that kind of brokenness would have sent her running. But Mikey... Mikey was different. Worth waiting for.

So, they drifted into a rhythm; quiet dinners, slow walks around the docks, late-night cafés, lazy Sunday lunches. Enough time together to grow something tender; enough restraint to pretend it meant nothing. When her sister started to sniff around the situation, Mikey suggested dinner, all four of them, somewhere neutral, Warrington maybe.

So, on a mild weekend in March 2000, the four of them found themselves eating pasta drowned in garlic butter, talking about kids and holidays and all the soft, unimportant things people use as camouflage.

Jamie's questions were clumsy, a little too pointed to be accidental but Mikey let them bounce off him.

"So Mikey, do you believe in all that astrology rubbish. She's well into it. Star signs and all that. I mean how can every Sagittarius in the world be like every other fucking Sagittarius? So what sign are you Mikey?...Gemini eh. Is that June?...Oh May, my pals' birthday is in May 16th, what's yours?...23rd, I'll have to remember that. We'll have a drink eh. How old will you be?"

Mikey saw it all. A fairly obvious way of getting his date of birth without directly asking for it. A nudge to some bent copper who'd run Mikey's name through the PNC, which suited him perfectly.

He would get word to Jock McAllister in the morning and they would identify if Mikey's name had been searched. If it had, the record they'd find was exactly what he needed them to find: a couple of possession convictions, a whiff of something bigger, rumours that Mikey Vaughan was a man on the rise.

The evening ended exactly the way he'd planned. A bit of play-fighting over the bill, then Alfonso, the proprietor himself, swooping in, kissing Mikey on both cheeks and declaring the meal 'a pleasure for an old friend'. The table froze.

Jamie's surprise was genuine. The glint in his eye was something else entirely.

'Who the hell was Mikey Vaughan?'

And that, that was the hook he'd been waiting for.

OVER THE NEXT FEW MONTHS, Mikey and Michelle drifted into a rhythm that felt dangerously close to comfort. The coffees and lunches stretched a little longer each time; the dinners ended later; the quiet walks along the docks became a habit neither of them commented on. When he told her he had "business" in the Midlands, she never pressed him, though the curiosity flickered in her eyes. She'd asked, once, what exactly he did for a living.

"Commodities," he'd said with a shrug that looked practiced, "I exploit financial opportunities in the commodities market."

It was artfully vague; just enough truth to steady the lie, just enough nonsense to discourage questions. Michelle had laughed softly and called it 'proper gobbledegook', but she didn't push. She liked him too much to risk looking nosy, and he liked her too much to give her anything real.

Jamie, however, wasn't quite so easily soothed. He'd wandered into the room one afternoon while Michelle and Sarah whispered about Mikey's mysterious work.

"Well, whatever it is," Sarah muttered, "He's doing alright. His exwife's rinsing him, but he's never short of money. And he stays in some very nice hotels for someone who's always apparently away on business."

Michelle added, almost protectively, "He's been stressed lately.

Something's gone wrong with a deal. He's worried."

Jamie lingered just long enough to catch the tone under the words —the guarded fondness, the unanswered questions. Then he strolled in fully, wearing that casual look he saved for moments when he was digging.

"Oh, hi, Michelle. Been thinking, we should have Mikey round for dinner again. Be good to see him. Why Don't you chat with Sarah and fix a date?"

The offer sounded warm enough, but Mikey would hear the message clearly when Michelle repeated it to him later.

Jamie Grant was circling. And the game was moving to its next phase.

BY THE TIME spring slid quietly into summer, Jamie had stopped kidding himself that Mikey Vaughan was just some bruised-hearted stray clinging to Michelle for comfort. There was more to him; layers, shadows, a certain worldliness that didn't quite fit the sob story he wore like an old coat. The man had scars, that much was clear, but they didn't look like the kind you pick up from marital strife. These were older, deeper, earned the hard way. He'd watched the way people nodded to Mikey in bars, subtle, deferential, and how meals vanished from bills with a wink from a proprietor who supposedly hadn't seen him in years. Even in Liverpool, where faces blurred and reputations were fickle, there were blokes who straightened up when Mikey walked past. That wasn't heartbreak. That was history.

His contact in the police had coughed up the bare bones: a couple of possession convictions, nothing spectacular. But behind that, buried in the usual murk of 'intel reports', were the whispers, suggestions that Vaughan was edging upwards in some circle or other. Commodities? Not the stock-market kind, whatever commodities Mikey had claimed to dabble in, it wasn't gambling on the FTSE. Something grittier. Something that made sense of those hotel stays, the expensive dinners, the nervous tension he'd been wearing. The occasional looks over his shoulder, like a man looking for a tail.

Jamie wasn't stupid. Mikey was interesting. Dangerous, perhaps, but interesting all the same. So, when Victor Harland called and told him to keep Vaughan close, Jamie didn't argue.

"Test him, if you like. Every man's got principles. I want to know what his are."

Just like that, the ground shifted beneath them. At the next family gathering Jamie played it casual, too casual, suggesting they "nipped out for an hour while the girls catch up." A couple of beers, a chin-wag, man talk.

Mikey smiled, nodded, played along. He'd been waiting for this.

"Okay if we go in your motor, Mikey? Mine needs new brake pads."

Of course it did.

Mikey's Subaru Impreza Turbo sat on the kerb outside, ice-blue paintwork, police-garage resurrection, plates tied neatly into his alias history. The sort of car that turned heads and pricked curiosity.

Jamie whistled low. "Do you get pulled driving this thing?"

"I don't thrash it," Mikey said, deadpan. "I usually get a police escort for a couple of miles, then they get bored and bugger off." Jamie laughed, but his eyes stayed sharp.

They climbed in. The night was mild, the engine a quiet growl beneath them.

"Mind if we swing by somewhere first?" Jamie asked as they pulled away, "Got a present to pick up. Need to drop it off after." A test, then. Mikey didn't blink.

"Tell me where I'm going."

Jamie directed him to a semi on the fringes of Toxteth. Mikey waited in the car while Jamie disappeared inside. Two minutes later he reemerged with a backpack bulging in that unmistakable way that had nothing to do with wrapping paper or ribbons. Birthday present, right.

Next stop: Croxteth. Another quick visit, another quiet exchange. The backpack vanished into a doorway, and an overstuffed brown envelope came back out. It landed in Jamie's jacket. Nothing discreet, it was meant to be seen.

"Right then. Pint?"

Later, back at Michelle and Sarah's, after the spaghetti bolognese (most of which the twins wore rather than ate) and after the girls drifted into the kitchen to gossip while the kids clattered upstairs, Jamie finally made his move.

A quick glance to ensure they were alone, then he pressed two neat dealer-folds into Mikey's hand, twenties, about two hundred quid.

"There you go, big man. Thanks for the help today."

Mikey tucked the cash into his pocket without counting it. "No worries. Happy to help a friend."

Jamie hesitated, the moment he'd been waiting for.

"You're not gonna ask what it was all about?"

Mikey shook his head. Calm. Uninterested. Exactly as a man of his supposed status should be.

"None of my business."

And Jamie saw it; the steadiness, the lack of fear, the quiet acceptance. The kind of man you could trust... or use.

The first test was over. Mikey had passed with distinction.

As the summer months moved towards autumn, there were a few more similar tests, packages that Mikey was trusted to pick up from a location and deliver to another, without Jamie being present. He never delved to see what he was carrying. He figured that was what they were testing - would he be tempted to probe? He had got rid of his Suburu and was now driving a "98 plate Cosworth, still punchy but less ostentatious than the previous car. That had been seen as a wise decision.

Victor Harland's name was mentioned a few times, and it was clear that Jamie was looking for Mikey's reaction. Yes, of course he'd heard the name, few hadn't. Yes, he'd heard the stories of violence and intimidation, but if you're at the top, you have to keep a control on things, or you won't be there long. Mikey said he would have exactly the same attitude if his business was as widespread as Harland's.

When Jamie had reported that back to Harland, they had both concluded that Mikey Vaughan sounded like he knew the score and that was almost certainly based on experience. He had connections - he knew people. Harland's only concern was why he wasn't 'seeing to' Michelle yet. 'Is he gay, or is there another reason?'

Jamie took a lot of delight in telling Mikey that Harland thought he was a 'woofter'.

Mikey would normally have winced at the use of such derogatory terminology, but instead he kept his smile fixed and his heartbeat steady. He gave as good as he got, a neat little insult flicked back across the table, harmless enough on the surface, sharp enough to land. But beneath the banter, beneath the mask, a colder truth pulsed. He was getting really close now - close enough that one wrong word could see him on the wrong side of a handgun, or potentially standing at Harland's shoulder, where he could learn everything he needed to in order to bring down Harland and destroy his organisation.

And that meant one thing. It was time to update Jock McAllister.

A MEETING WAS ARRANGED at a safe location. Jock listened intently. The old Scot was pleased with how much progress Mikey had made, but there was clearly one doubt in his mind.

"Do you think he means it, the jibe? Or is it just banter? There are stories about Harland—gay-bashing when he was a lad. Got worse as he got older. Maybe he changed. Maybe he didn't. What do you reckon?"

Mikey stared at nothing for a long moment. It was a question he couldn't answer.

"I don't know, boss," he admitted quietly. "I'll just have to hope it's all bollocks."

Jock looked him squarely in the eye.

"Hope? I learned a long time ago that it's the hope that destroys you. I've been hoping for a break on Harland for too long. We can't leave anything to chance. To hope. Time to cross that bridge".

"Are you asking me to do what I think you are. To sacrifice my values and to potentially break the law just to remove a barrier that we are not even certain exists?"

Jock leaned back and fixed Mikey with that granite stare of his, the kind that made you feel weighed, measured, and catalogued.

"I can't order you to step over that line," he said quietly, "Christ knows, it's a line no sane man should cross. What you do from here — that's on you son. Your call. Always has been."

He rubbed a hand across his jaw, the scrape of stubble loud in the silence, "But listen to me, Mikey... we're never going to get this close again. Not to him. Not to bringing down a man who's left more wreckage in his wake than a winter tide. This, " he tapped the table with his forefinger, "...this is as near as we'll ever be to shutting the bastard down for good."

He let the words hang for a second or two. Then his voice softened, and once again he was the Jock McAllister that had first sought Mick's help.

"Maybe we keep going and it all falls our way. Maybe it doesn't. It's a gamble I can't make on your behalf. But whatever you decide... you need to hear this."

He leaned forward, forearms on the desk, eyes unblinking.

"You'll always have my respect. My support. Whatever comes of this, good, bad, or biblical, I'm with you. I won't let you stand alone out there." A long pause and then, "I've got your back. God help us both."

The following weekend, Mikey vanished 'on business'. In truth, he was in Birmingham, collecting jewellery and props, five grand authorised by Jock, with one exception. A small 18-carat necklace with a heart pendant. He'd paid for that one himself. Not for the job.

Not for Harland. For Michelle. A genuine token from a man who wasn't supposed to feel a thing. Except he did.

Mikey had wondered whether Michelle might like a quiet escape for her thirty-second. Nothing flashy, just a couple of nights in the Lakes where the air was clean enough to pretend life made sense.

They checked into a suite at the Barrow Dale Hotel on the morning of her birthday, 4th November. When the receptionist smiled and welcomed Mr. and Mrs. Vaughan, Michelle shot him a sideways look, half-question, half-secret pleasure.

"It really is my birthday," she whispered, to herself.

Outside, Derwent Water lay crisp and still under an autumn sky, all copper light and cold breath, but neither of them cared much for scenery just then.

Once they crossed that line, truly crossed it, days of restraint collapsed into something fierce, hungry, and long overdue. They barely let go of each other.

Later, while Michelle showered before dinner, steam curling under the bathroom door, Mikey sat on the edge of the bed and told the empty room a truth he couldn't tell her.

"One day she'll know what I am, and maybe she'll never forgive me... but God help me, I'm going to ask her to marry me. Whatever happens, she needs to know how I felt."

First a meal. Then a toast. Then her gift. When she saw the pendant he'd bought, a slim gold chain, a small heart that caught the light, she touched it like it was something precious, something meant. She wore it immediately; fingers brushing it every few minutes as though reminding herself it was real. Her eyes softened. He knew the words she was about to speak before her lips even parted.

Mikey glanced at his watch, stretched theatrically, and said lightly —far too lightly for the storm he felt inside, "Well... I don't know about you, but this fresh air and countryside has fairly worn me out."

She responded, "Hopefully not too much".

If it had been a calculated ploy, some cold, tactical move to take down a barrier no one was even sure was there, it certainly worked. Not that Mikey saw it that way. To him it wasn't strategy; it was consequence, and not one he'd planned on.

Still, something shifted after that weekend. People looked at him differently. You could feel it in the slight pauses, the longer glances, the marks of recalculation happening behind friendly smiles.

Jamie's tone was the biggest tell. A softness now and then, sure, maybe the lad looked at Mikey as future family, but every so often a question carried a different weight, something probing under the varnish.

"You've got connections, haven't you, Mikey? Know some useful people, I'm told."

Mikey gave the shrug of a man who'd been asked versions of that question all his life.

"I don't know who's been telling tales, but yeah, I know a few people."

Jamie leaned in, voice dipped low, "You know anyone who might handle a small job for a friend of a friend?"

"That depends," Mikey said, careful, casual, "What kind of job are we talking about?"

"A few bob needs sending overseas. There's a fella in the 'dam waiting on it. This friend of a friend would take it himself, but... well... he's got one of those faces. Attracts the wrong sort of attention. So we're after a courier. Don't suppose you know anyone?"

Mikey let the silence stretch, just long enough.

"What are we calling a few bob?"

"Three hundred grand".

"Yeah... I could find someone. Or," he added, almost lazily, "I could do it myself."

Jamie's grin held both relief and confirmation. "Hoped you'd say that."

MICK KNEW Amsterdam the way other men knew their childhood backstreets. Birmingham aside, it was the only place he could move through half asleep and still find his footing. So when Jamie hinted, clumsily, that Michelle might tag along, Mick brushed it aside with a line that only burnished his legend further.

"I don't take women on business," he said flatly, "Wrong time of the month and they'll blab everything to their mates. Keep women and work separate."

It was crude, ugly even, but it was exactly what men like Jamie expected from a bloke like Mikey Vaughan. The sort of line that earned respect in the wrong circles and doubt in the right ones.

But it was Jock McAllister's worries that gnawed at him. The old Scotsman had been turning the problem over like a hot stone: how to get European police to "randomly" stop Mikey, seize the cash, and make it look clean, all without blowing months of groundwork.

Mikey cut him off before the idea even found its legs.

"You do that, Jock, and it's over for me. They won't buy 'random '. Not for a second. I'll be marked as a grass, police, or I'll be seen as having nicked the money myself. Either way, I'm done."

The words hung between them like smoke. Jock knew it was true. He'd seen enough operations thwarted by an over-clever plan. There followed a verbal shuffle, half argument, half resignation, before Jock finally nodded, jaw tight.

"Fine. You deliver it. I'll speak to the Attorney General. We'll get you indemnified. You'll be covered, at least in the eyes of the law."

Legal permission to commit a crime. Another line crossed. Mikey said nothing. He just gave a slow nod, the kind a man gives when he's already too far in to climb back out.

TRAIN JOURNEYS SUITED HIM. Time folded out quietly in front of him —no disguises to wear, no lies to shape, just a seat by the window and space to let the mind wander.

He'd thumb through a book, drift through a bit of music, or play a private version of the old game show: What's My Line? A man in dungarees, boots scuffed, hands with callouses—builder of some sort, but no mortar splashes, pencil parked behind the ear... carpenter, most likely.

A round-faced woman, immaculate apron stuffed into her tote, blue plaster clinging to one finger, cook or baker.

Teenager with the tight haircut, the huge Bergens, posture straight enough to balance a glass; military, almost certainly.

A couple of medical students judging by the pens in their pockets, the briefcases bulging with books, and just the look of very junior doctors.

He never found out if he'd guessed right. Didn't matter. It passed the miles and kept his mind busy.

Train to King's Cross St Pancras, Eurostar to Brussels, Thalys up to Amsterdam Centraal; eight, maybe nine hours door to door. Mikey barely noticed the time.

Long journeys were second nature now; they gave him space to watch, listen, file things away.

By the time he stepped out into the Dutch cold he'd already clocked half a dozen faces he'd never forget and half a dozen more he could afford to.

The Park Plaza Victoria was only a short walk from the station, a slab of warmth and glass against the winter bite. Check in, two bags upstairs; one backpack with a few clothes and toiletries, one nylon sports bag with three hundred grand zipped inside. Room service, curtains drawn. He wasn't letting that money out of his sight, not for anyone.

He phoned Michelle the moment he arrived, though he was quietly grateful when the line cracked and died under the weight of bad roaming. She deserved better than clipped answers and half-truths. He told himself he'd make it right later. He used to tell himself that about Bernie.

The next morning he'd just started on his continental breakfast when the mobile buzzed. Jamie's voice came clean as a whistle down the line—too clean for this side of Europe.

"Mikey. Coffee at the Bluey Teehwis in Vondelpark. Someone'll meet you. Don't forget your sports gear." And that was that.

Mick—not Mikey—had drunk cappuccinos at the Blauwe Thee-huis before, in warmer months when the place spilled blue chairs into the park like confetti.

December was a different story. Bare branches, cold stone, and an interior so empty the echoes felt personal. He chose a table with his back to the door, ordered another cappuccino, and let the quiet settle.

Only a few minutes passed and he was aware that someone had interrupted the immediate peace. Footsteps. A man's voice, Scouse and confident.

"No thank you. I'm here to meet my friend over there."

Mikey didn't turn. He stared through the window, pretending to study the grey sky reflected in the pond outside.

"Hello Mikey. Nice to finally meet you."

Without looking up, Mikey responded, "Good to meet you. Is it Vic or Victor?"

A low chuckle followed by, "Jamie said you were quick. It's Victor. 'Vic' is that spray that gets up your nose."

Mikey got to his feet and shook the man's hand. Harland's grip was firm without trying to prove anything. The suit, dark grey, immaculate, was expensive in a way that whispered, not shouted. His hair was cropped and bleached to a pale gold that made those eyes even colder. And Christ, those eyes... deep, icy blue, the colour of frozen lakes. He'd seen eyes like that before; bikers, gangsters, para-militaries, men who'd taken another man's life without a second thought. But Harland smiled easily, almost warmly, and Mikey felt that old instinct rise: the knack of making dangerous men relax around him. It was a gift, or a defect, depending on who you asked.

"Appreciate you helping out. I've got to run, this needs delivering sharpish. I'll tell Jamie to sort you out. I think you'll be pleased. Might have a job for you soon, if you're keen."

"I should have some time free," Mikey snapped back.

"You don't want to know what the job is?"

"What, and spoil the excitement?"

Harland grinned, scooped up the sports bag from beside Mikey's feet and said, smiling, "Jamie vouches for you. Don't make him look a tit." Then he tapped the side of his nose with his forefinger and pointed the finger firmly at Mikey...a silent, 'I know who you are'.

Mikey knew though, it wasn't that Harland knew who he was, it's that Harland felt that he had got the measure of Mikey and that Mikey had measured up well.

Back at the Park Plaza, Mikey packed at speed, paid the bill, and slipped into the churn of Centraal Station. With luck he'd be in Brussels before sunset and in London by midnight. He let the train rock him into stillness, eyes closing for a moment, just a moment.

When he opened them, he caught sight of two familiar faces on the platform. The same two 'medical students' from his journey the day before. One of them, Hugh Grant's younger brother, kept fiddling with his ear as if checking a bud that wasn't there. They weren't students. They weren't even punters. Surveillance cops, clear as day. What the hell was McAllister playing at?

11

CLIMBING THE LADDER

J ust before Christmas 2000, Mikey and Michelle took a flat overlooking the water at the Royal Albert Dock; glass, brick, and winter lights reflecting off the Mersey. To Michelle it felt like a fresh start; to Mikey it was a convenience. He made the case to Jock easily enough: being in Liverpool placed him closer to the pulse of Harland's empire, and if Harland trusted him now, proximity could only help. Jock agreed, though not with his usual enthusiasm. He pressed for a timeline, an oddly naïve question from a man usually too shrewd to ask it.

"Look, I'm making good progress, boss. When we started, time wasn't the issue. If it had been, I'd never have made it this far. If I rush things now, try to push deeper too fast, Harland will smell it a mile off. We can't spook him. I promise, I'll get you your evidence."

Jock listened, jaw working, eyes colder than the wind off the Mersey.

"Mikey," he said at last, "I want Harland behind bars. And I'll be straight with you... if I have to put you in the witness box to get that conviction, I will."

There was no bluff there. Mikey felt it. Jock wanted a scalp, and he didn't particularly care whose fingers got caught in the door on the way to it.

Mick knew, as every U/C knows, one day the mask might have to come off. Mick had testified before; hidden behind a screen, alias name not his own, a judge provided with proof that 'the witness is a serving police officer'.

But even then, there were always consequences. Access agents compromised. Innocent bystanders leaned on. Lives bent or broken. This time the price was bigger. If Michelle ever discovered who, and what, he was, the fallout wouldn't just be professional. It would be personal, devastatingly so. Jock knew that, but he'd waved it aside with the usual platitude about 'crossing that bridge'.

"Boss, if I have to give evidence, I have to give evidence. But give me a bit longer. Maybe we won't need that nuclear option."

What surprised Mikey wasn't the threat, it was the tone behind it. Jock had changed. Impatience had crept in where once there had been calculation. A tremor in the certainty. A man watching the clock run down.

What's going on?

The question hung between them, unanswered.

OVER CHRISTMAS and into the fresh, crisp days of the new year, something in their life together settled into place with the ease of a pair of hands finally finding the right gloves.

Michelle adored him, almost embarrassingly so at times, and, God help him, he found himself depending on that warmth far more than was wise.

She trusted him without hesitation, without question, without the faintest whisper of doubt. And he, leaning on the old, well-worn pain of a betrayal that wasn't quite his, fed her a past stitched from borrowed truths: a bruised childhood; a father with fists for hands; leaving home too young; the wandering years; the strange safety of a biker crew; the climb back up; the small-time hustles that grew into a 'business'. Storylines he understood well enough to tell without blinking.

She listened, gently, carefully, probing not out of suspicion but out of care. Curiously, the one place she never wandered into was his 'business dealings'. She gave that part of his life a wide berth. At first he'd found it odd; later, he realised she simply knew better than to ask.

In return, Michelle opened her own past to him, piece by piece, like someone unwrapping an old wound to let the air reach it.

He could picture the little mixed-race girl in 1970s Liverpool, sitting on the concrete steps of the 'Bullring', the local nickname for the St Andrews Gardens tenements, brave face sobbing quietly after another round of playground cruelty.

She told him about the city's tensions, factory closures, lost jobs, stale resentment in the air, and the police racism that eventually boiled over into the Toxteth riots.

She spoke of school, where numbers had been her escape the way words had once been his. That talent had nudged open a door, led her towards accountancy, and away from the shadows of St Andrews Gardens.

Then she told him about Dennis O'Grady, 'Dog' to his mates. Eighteen, dazzled by an Irish smile and a mechanic's swagger; the whirlwind romance; the marriage; the dream of a family, shattered by the quiet grief of her inability to have kids. And then his drinking. The backhanded slaps. The bruises. The final straw, and the frantic flight to her sister's spare room.

Jamie and his mates had sorted the man out after that, old-fashioned justice, the sort you didn't report but remembered.

O'Grady vanished, and Michelle kept his name simply because changing it back had felt like too much trouble.

Now, though, she looked at Mikey with something soft and tremulous in her eyes.

"I was going to change it," she said quietly, fingers twisting the chain at her throat, "But... maybe there's another option? Would me not being able to have children be a problem? Because if it is, I'd rather know now."

Her voice barely reached him, but the question hit him square in the chest. And for the first time in years, the great Mikey Vaughan, storyteller, operator, professional liar, found himself struggling for words.

OVER THE MONTHS THAT FOLLOWED, Mikey slipped into Harland's world with the sort of ease that should have troubled him more than it did. At first, he was just another pair of hands, useful for carrying cash across postcodes, a courier with enough nerve to avoid flinching at the wrong moment. Cocaine? That was someone else's department.

Harland didn't fix what wasn't broken. But with Mikey, he sensed potential. A man people would listen to. A man other men might fear. It didn't take long for that reputation to take shape. A few late payers, a few quiet door knocks on the warming spring and summer evenings, and Mikey found himself delivering reminders with a level tone and a stillness behind the eyes that made people rethink their priorities. No shouting, no fists, no theatre—just a cold, reasoned promise of what might happen if they didn't fall into line. And it worked. Word spread. Mikey Vaughan wasn't a man you crossed. Not twice.

Behind the scenes, he kept feeding the machine. Coded notes scribbled in his flat at 3 a.m. while Michelle slept soundly; names, phone numbers, dates, cash transfers, supply routes, muttered conversations with Harland. All of it packaged neatly, passed to McAllister in ways that made the evidence admissible. Useful, incriminating. But not enough. Not nearly enough.

Jock wanted the treasure trove; the money, the accounts, the assets buried under a mountain of shell names and offshore lies. When Harland fell, McAllister wanted him stripped bare: cars gone, houses seized, bank accounts frozen solid. He wanted to break him.

To keep the pressure on, Jock had quietly nudged a local drug squad DI to make enquiries about the Brummie lad running with Harland. West Midlands intelligence was only too happy to help: slippery, violent, linked to two gangland murders, never proven but probable.

Exactly the sort of whispers a man like Harland respected. The rumours seeped back through the grapevine in no time, landing in Victor Harland's ear, exactly as intended.

Harland's demeanour changed almost overnight. A new stillness, a flicker of acknowledgment, respect, even. In Mikey, he saw a man cut from the same cold cloth as himself. Someone you wanted at your shoulder, not on the other side of a locked door. And then the invitations began. Not errands. Meetings. Not orders. Questions. "We've got a cash-flow problem with this lad. What's your take, Mikey?"

The outcome was usually the same: Mikey at a doorstep, hands in pockets, voice soft as smoke. He'd explain the situation, the consequences, the timetable. The debtors dropped quickly into line. They always did. And each time, Harland took note.

Each time, Mikey stepped one rung higher up the ladder of Harland's empire, and one rung deeper into the abyss. And each time, he told himself it was just the job, the cost of getting close enough to bring a monster down.

But the line between duty and damnation was getting thinner by the day.

By the autumn of 2001, the shine had started to dull. Even Jock McAllister, normally all granite and grit, was letting unease show through the cracks. At their latest meet, he'd leaned forward across the Formica table, voice pitched low, as if naming the fear too loudly might make it real.

"Mikey, you're still one of us. I hope you remember that. I need you pulling out every stop you've got. Find the smoking gun. I don't care how you do it, I need those ledgers. The money's what'll bring him down. He still trusts you, doesn't he?"

Jock wasn't wrong to worry. Local drug squad whispers painted a picture of a man who'd climbed the ladder faster than anyone expected. Harland's crew spoke Mikey's name with the kind of respect earned only through blood or fear, or both. And Harland himself had begun to treat him like a brother, albeit one who might still need watching.

"You've become a person of interest," Harland had warned him one night, swirling a glass of something expensive and amber, "Make sure you watch your back."

Mikey had offered the same easy shrug he'd given villains, handlers, and lovers alike.

"I'm always careful."

And Harland believed him. He always did. So much so that through the autumn he kept Mikey away from the dirty work, collecting debts, shifting cash, oiling the machinery of intimidation. Harland insisted on using other lads for the heavy lifting.

"No need to risk you," he'd said.

And that single sentence told Mikey everything: he wasn't just being trusted. He was being protected.

Tom O'Dowd had joked one night that the boss had developed a crush on Mikey, right up until Devlin cuffed him around the head and muttered, "Christ, Tommy, don't let him hear that. You know how he gets about the gayers."

Devlin, Harland's long-time lieutenant, had one foot already in Marbella, lining up a villa and the kind of sunshine that warmed the blood and bleached the past. Harland had given his blessing; better to have one of his own holding court in Spain.

But Devlin's exit left a vacuum. An unofficial vacancy. A new second-in-command needed to be chosen. And Mikey, quick-climbing, soft-spoken, dangerous when necessary Mikey, was suddenly the man everyone was watching. The man Harland was watching most of all. Well, except for Jock McAllister.

Another Christmas was approaching quickly, and he had tasked the local NCS team with beginning an investigation into Victor Harland and his team, despite his well-founded beliefs that the man had some cops in his pocket.

The covert meetings with Mikey continued and, to all intents and purposes, Jock was content, for now, to continue to receive the steady flow of evidence that would help incriminate Harland.

"I've probably been a bit too demanding at times, son, but I do appreciate everything that you're doing, putting your neck on the line every single day. You are doing a grand job, keep plugging away, and keep looking for the money. But for now, enjoy Christmas. How is that lovely lady of yours? Is she well?"

Apart from Jock previously describing her as "the bridge that must be crossed," he had never before asked about her health or welfare.

Why now?

12

ALL IS QUIET

Christmas gave Mikey a breather, a chance to drag some air into lungs that had been tight for months. The flat he shared with Michelle had become more than a bolt hole; it was a sanctuary, a world where he could hang up the mask for a few blessed hours. There were two Mikey Vaughans now, and both were dangerously believable. Michelle got the gentle one, the easy laugh, the warm arm around her waist, the bloke who made her feel safe. Harland got the other: the man with the cold voice, the steady hands, the one people crossed the street to avoid.

Mick Dorrington, the real man beneath the paper names, was little more than a ghost drifting in the spaces in between.

Harland had gifted him a Jaeger-LeCoultre Master Compressor for Christmas, a watch so new it wasn't supposed to exist yet. A few grand at least, and heavy with the weight of trust, or ownership.

Mikey logged it, like he logged every packet of cash, every favour, every murmur that might later become evidence. Michelle never asked about the notebooks he kept tucked away; she understood instinctively that whatever he did was better left unexamined.

January thawed into routine. Mikey was permanently at Harland's shoulder now, a shadow for all the wrong reasons. That was how he was finally ushered into the 'Night Council', a whispered myth among Harland's men. Now he knew it was real.

They met at three in the morning in an abandoned office block that smelled of damp plaster and rotting floorboards. Mikey memorised every corridor, every emergency exit, every face. He'd pass the layout to Jock at the next meet.

Talk drifted across the dusty table: a springtime importation, a shipment bigger than any they'd run before. Harland handed out fresh burners, metal clattering quietly as pistols were exchanged like party favours. Mikey nodded at the right points, asked nothing, watched everything. Harland trusted him, that was the real danger.

A week later Harland called an impromptu gathering, just the inner circle. He looked almost relaxed. That alone set Mikey on edge. Harland talked about accounts being healthy, very healthy.

He'd always promised that the men who backed him would retire wealthy, and now, he said, it was time to start imagining those futures. Keep it modest, he warned. No neon-lit Lamborghinis, no penthouses with glass balconies.

"Get your stories straight. I'll have someone to help with that... later."

It sounded like a farewell, like a curtain lowering on a long, brutal play. But it was the last meeting in late May 2002 that chilled Mikey to the bone.

Harland clapped him on the back and said he should take a couple of weeks off.

"Take Michelle somewhere warm. Caribbean if you fancy it. I'll sort your bonus, check the letterbox."

Too casual. Too generous. Too final.

Every instinct Mikey had honed, through biker bars, drug dens, and a hundred tense rooms where one wrong sentence could be a death warrant, prickled at once.

Something was off. Something was coming. Danger or paranoia, he couldn't yet tell the difference. But he did know one thing: he needed to get home to Michelle, pack a suitcase, and get her some-where safe.

Somewhere far from the Caribbean.

13

STRIKE

Local and national news outlets would all later roll out the same blunt headlines: a dawn blitz, dozens arrested, drugs and guns swept up in a coordinated strike stretching from Merseyside across to the Midlands. A triumph for the National Crime Squad, they'd say. A hammer blow to organised crime. A neat statement, polished for the cameras. Thankfully, no mention of an undercover operation.

At 5:30 a.m. on the first of June, while doors were splintering across the region, Mikey Vaughan was not some mythic lieutenant in a smoky backroom. He was standing barefoot and naked in the half-dark bedroom of his apartment at the Royal Albert Dock, watching the sky bruise into morning over the still water. Michelle was curled in the bed beside him, breathing softly, still adrift in whatever dream had claimed her.

He hadn't slept. His nerves hummed with the kind of warning he'd learned never to ignore. Fight or flight, only there was nothing left to fight and nowhere safe to fly.

Florida. He kept seeing that word in his head. Florida, or anywhere warm and far, somewhere he could take her before the tide turned. Just not the Caribbean.

He'd tell Jock on the way to the airport. Tell him why. He rehearsed the call in his mind. He thought he'd get up, make coffee, clear his head.

Then, he heard it in the corridor outside. A sound that didn't belong. A breath of movement. A whisper of something heavy shifting outside the flat.

Two seconds later the front door didn't so much break as explode, torn off its hinges in a thunderous blast that ripped through the stillness.

Shouts, boots, the sharp barks of dogs, the clatter of metal on metal. The whole room convulsed as armed officers poured in. And oddly, brutally, his first feeling was relief.

At least it's the good guys.

Orders cracked through the air.

"Armed police! Stay where you are - turn around - hands above your head! Are you armed?"

Mikey almost laughed. A short, humorless puff of breath.

"I'm completely naked," he said, "Of course I'm not armed."

They cuffed him anyway, fast, clinical, impersonal.

A policewoman, unseen until her voice broke through the din, had Michelle by the arm. Not rough, but firm. Firm enough. She didn't bother to look at Mikey.

"What's going on, Mikey?" Her voice carried a tremor that twisted something inside him.

"I'm sure," he said, forcing calm he didn't feel, "these good people will explain."

Of course they wouldn't. Not properly. Not in a way that would save her.

The firearms officers peeled away in practiced formation, leaving the room full of uniforms. Someone assisted him into a pair of joggers , small mercies.

Then came that voice. The soft Edinburgh lilt that had once sounded like sanctuary.

"Thank you, ladies and gents." Detective Superintendent John McAllister stepped forward, unreadable as stone, before continuing,

"Mikey Vaughan. I am executing an international arrest warrant on behalf of the Netherlands Police. You are under arrest for offences of money laundering. You do not have to say anything..."

Mikey almost smiled. It was bitter, but it was real.

An international arrest warrant. Nice touch, Jock. It would explain his sudden disappearance. It would keep the myth intact, but it wasn't the right time. Not by a long shot. Why the hell had Jock pulled the trigger now?

"And Michelle O "Grady..."

Mikey's stomach turned cold. Jock kept talking, voice steady.

"You are under arrest for concealing or transferring the proceeds of drug trafficking... assisting another to retain the benefit of drug trafficking... all contrary to the Drug Trafficking Act 1994. You do not have to say anything..."

She stood still, barefoot, hair tangled, eyes wide and shining. She didn't protest. Didn't plead. She just let the words wash over her and turned her head just enough to give Mikey a small, sad smile. She was allowed to dress, under supervision, and then they led her away. No struggle. No fuss. Her sad eyes fixed on Mikey until she disappeared behind a line of uniforms.

Once she was gone, they uncuffed him long enough to throw on a shirt and trainers. Then the steel bit his wrists again and two officers took him by the arms. As they guided him toward the ruined doorway, he heard Jock's voice snap like a whip behind him.

"Right—turn this place upside down. You know what we're looking for. Get on with it."

Mikey didn't look back. There was nothing left behind him worth saving.

MIKEY DIDN'T KNOW the two NCS officers who were ferrying him to wherever it was he was supposed to be going. They weren't talkers, no chit-chat, no sideways glances, none of the usual "you alright, mate?" that seasoned cops slip in when they're trying to keep an operation human. So he stayed in character, Mikey Vaughan; international villain, cool customer, no questions asked.

The silence pressed in, gave him too much room to think. The raid. The cuffs. Michelle's terrified eyes. He kept telling himself her arrest was nothing more than a clean extraction, a way to get her out while the team scrubbed the flat of everything that smelled like him.

He pictured her returning to a ghost home, his ghost life gone, no trace but the indentation his absence would leave behind. Maybe she'd panic, maybe she'd rage, maybe she'd grieve. And eventually, someone would whisper that Vaughan had died in some foreign cell, nameless and broken. He'd died before. It was a trick he knew how to play. But Michelle... losing her would hurt him. Even more than losing Bernie had.

Funny how a man could fake a dozen names but couldn't fake the way one woman got under his ribs. In another lifetime, they'd have grown old together. But this wasn't that lifetime, and this wasn't that world.

The car rolled into a sterile yard behind a modern office block in some industrial pocket of Stoke-on-Trent. He was moved to the back of a Transit with blacked-out windows...anonymous space, anonymous men.

The driver explained, flat as cardboard, that they were taking him to the Midlands where he'd 'need to be held' until a full debrief could be arranged.

Held? The word snagged. He wasn't being treated as a flight risk anymore, but he was still under caution, still technically a criminal. The suit riding shotgun didn't say a single word. The whole thing had the slick feel of competence, yet underneath it, something felt off. Too controlled. Too careful.

They stopped at Hilton Park. A toilet break, a Greggs pasty shoved his way. He accepted it; instinct told him to keep his energy up.

The van moved off again before the pastry was half eaten. The men weren't hostile, but they weren't allies either. Just professionals doing a job he wasn't entirely sure he recognised anymore.

Then the confusion crept in, slow and unwelcome. He'd been in tight spots before, walked through fire with nothing but a lie between him and death. But this, this grey corridor of silence, these faceless escorts, the absence of explanation, this felt different.

For the first time in a long time, Mikey wondered if he was the only one who didn't know how the next scene played out.

The modern office block, a peripheral part of the NEC complex sour of Birmingham, was all red steel and darkened windows, stylish enough to pass for a corporate hub, anonymous enough to hide anything. There were no signs shouting 'police', but the heavy security gates, the guards who didn't bother with friendliness, and the keypads that blinked like watchful eyes told a different story entirely. Mick knew of a few of these quiet government bolt holes, scattered across the Midlands like buried secrets, and he realised, with a dull churn in his gut, that he'd probably reached the centre of one.

They guided him into a large interview suite—every inch of it designed for conversations people should never overhear. A thick oak table sat square in the middle, four chairs surrounding it, solid but softened with those institutional cushions no one ever found comfortable. A twin-tape recorder sat poised between two microphones. Beside it, a laminated PACE rights sheet in three languages, just in case the suspect didn't speak English or didn't want to. Pens and fresh pads of lined paper were neatly arranged as though awaiting a meeting that no one really wanted to happen. In the corner stood a water dispenser stacked with untouched cups. On one wall stretched a long two-way mirror, silent, opaque, watching. The whole room smelt faintly of disinfectant and tension.

His escorts told him politely to make himself comfortable. Then they vanished.

An hour bled away in silence. Mick spent it slumped forward, staring at the grain of the table, trying to make sense of... well, anything. Nothing added up. Nothing even tried to.

When the door finally opened, Jock McAllister entered with two men in dark suits who carried themselves like judges, or executioners.

The shift in the air hit Mick first. Jock wasn't smiling.

"I guess today has been a bit of a shock," Jock began, voice low, almost rehearsed, "We had to keep it like that. I'll explain."

He gave the outline—raids across Liverpool, evidence of drug trafficking, firearms, and even a conspiracy to murder. They believed Mick had been the intended target. They'd "had to act quickly." They "couldn't appraise him beforehand." Jock apologised, but it landed with the weight of a formality.

The two suits watched him closely, as if waiting for him to crack, or at least blink. Mick opened his mouth to ask... something, anything... but the words tangled and died. Better to keep his powder dry until he understood the battlefield.

One of the suits then explained that there was a necessity to conduct an interview under caution with Mick. He leant forward and switched on the tape-recording machine. He spoke slowly and deliberately.

"I am Superintendent John Porter. With me is...."

"Sergeant Dave Price."

"And also present is..."

"Superintendent Jock McAllister."

Each of the names spoken by its owner, for the benefit of the tape recording.

Porter then addressed Mick, "Could you confirm your name please, for the tape?"

Mick hesitated a fraction too long. Who was he?

"My birth name is Michael Richard Dorrington... but I've usually been known as Mick Dorrington."

"Michael Richard Dorrington, I am arresting you on suspicion of conspiracy to import controlled drugs, and also of money laundering offences under the Drug Trafficking Act. You do not have to say anything, unless you wish to do so, but what you do say may be recorded and given in evidence. This interview is being recorded and the time is now......"

He went on to give the time and date, again confirming the other occupants in the room, and then asked the question that Mick had been anticipating. "Would you like your legal representative to be present during this interview? If you would, you can either choose your own representative or we can provide an independent legal representative, or on your behalf. Alternatively, you could request the representation from the Police Federation."

Another long period of thought.

"Right now I am happy to proceed, but I may need to ask for legal representation at any point in the future." He felt more off-balance than he allowed to show.

No legal representation. It surprised them. Truth be told, it surprised him too. They pushed on.

They referred to evidence of his involvement in a two-year conspiracy to supply cocaine.

"That sounds about right," Mick replied.

Evidence of laundering drug proceeds.

"That is indeed true." And then the hook.

"Conspiring with Michelle O'Grady to launder the proceeds of drug trafficking."

"Not true. She was not involved, In anything."

"Names of co-conspirators?"

Mick sat upright, steady now, clear now.

"Of course. I entered into a criminal conspiracy at the direct request of Detective Superintendent Jock McAllister, with the aim of disrupting an ongoing conspiracy by Victor Harland and his associates. Michelle O'Grady was not one of those associates. I understand that an indemnity from prosecution issued by the Attorney General was obtained by Superintendent McAllister... and that he can provide the supporting evidence that I passed to him throughout the operation. I will not answer any further questions without legal representation. In fact, I won't be answering any more questions, full stop."

The silence that followed was thick enough to chew. Porter opened his briefcase, took out a document, and read the terms of suspension, clinical, exhaustive, suffocating. Full pay, but no contact with serving officers. No setting foot in police premises. No leaving the UK. No discussing the case. Available for interview at any time. Sign here.

He signed.

Porter asked if he had any questions. He shook his head.

"No, sir. Thank you."

The suits left. Then Jock paused at the door. Six words. Soft. True. Almost kind.

"Do not try and contact her."

It wasn't a threat. It wasn't even an instruction. It was mercy. Mick nodded—because anything else would have broken him.

THERE WAS AT LEAST a rhythm to being shoved onto 'gardening leave', if you could call keeping your head down while wondering whether a contract was out on you a rhythm. It didn't exactly encourage nights out. Instead, Mick settled for quiet evening walks along the canals, the water turned murky gold as the days stretched into summer. And summer soon became Autumn. He lived in a constant hum of vigilance. He'd always been observant, but now even the mundane looked like it had teeth.

He kept trying to join the dots, to build the picture nobody would show him. Jock hadn't asked a single question about the evidence Mikey had spent two years collecting. He hadn't asked him to verify a scrap of the notes that must have been recovered from the flat he'd shared with Michelle.

It felt as if they were hoping, praying, to secure convictions without touching anything that had come through Mikey's hands. But why? That had been Mick's bloody purpose. He'd gambled everything to get that evidence. So why bury it?

Maybe Harland had twigged. If he'd sniffed that Mikey was a source, an informant, maybe even an undercover cop, then why not get him providing the crucial nails for Harlands coffin. There was no access agent, no snitch to protect. Surely, if Harland knew that Mikey was going to testify, he'd try a bit of plea bargaining.

Unless, of course, they thought Mikey had gone bad. Crossed the line. You couldn't exactly put your faith in a man you were about to charge with serious drug and money-laundering offences.

A defence brief would eat him alive. Easier, then, to shove him in the dock as well, another bent cop brought down. Or, more convenient yet, sweep him under the carpet and pretend he'd never existed.

There was another possibility; they were protecting themselves. An undercover cop sleeping with the enemy, now that was scandal. The sort that set tabloids alight and got officers suspended, sacked, or quietly buried.

Yes, Jock would want to keep his own suit clean. It had been a long road, one Mick hadn't wanted but had been pulled down all the same.

There had been highs, little victories, worming his way into a major criminal network from a cold start. No introduction, no reference, just that chance meeting on Millennium Eve. Except..., hang on, how much of a chance was it? That clumsy step on his toe. The pretty girl with the lethal smile, sister-in-law to one of Harland's trusted lieutenants. In a huge crowd of 250,000 people.

"Of all the toes, in all the world, you had to step on mine."

Michelle's face flashed back to him, the soft, sad smile as the police led her away. No panic. No outrage. Almost as if she'd been expecting it. And she had never once asked what he really did when he was gone for hours, or why he spent so much time with Jamie or Harland. Not once.

Perhaps she already knew.

Jock's words rose up like cold breath on his neck, 'Do not try and contact her'. Not for operational reasons. Not for his own safety. But maybe because he wouldn't like what he found.

And then it clicked, the most likely reason Jock didn't need Mikey's evidence: he already had everything he required. The picture sharpened, slow and ugly.

Jock McAllister had leverage over Michelle O'Grady, Harland's accountant. She'd said she worked in 'accounts', nothing more. The understatement of the century.

A carefully staged 'chance' meeting with Mikey, knowing exactly the persona he'd be wearing. Maybe she had been directed where to go by a surveillance team that he hadn't been looking for.

Jamie introduced soon after, of course. And Michelle, playing her part, nudging him along with that nonsense about him being gay, not because Harland cared, but because she needed Mikey drawn closer, tangled up.

And when the dust settled, the accounting books would be the real kill shot. Harland's entire empire written in ledgers and balance sheets.

Michelle would receive a tidy little letter from Jock, her cooperation noted, her sentence softened.

And Mikey Vaughan?

He was the patsy. The expendable cog. The reason everything had gone tits-up. Michelle would walk away clean. No reprisals. No loose ends.

And Mick Dorrington, whatever was left of him, would be left alone with the bitter taste of betrayal.

Again

14

OH, WHAT A TANGLED WEB WE WEAVE

Sometimes Mick laughed at his own stupidity, short, bitter barks that echoed off the canal like stones skipping on dark water. Other times the laugh caught in his throat and turned into something else. Anger. Shame. Grief. It rolled through him in waves.

You live by the sword, you die by the sword. And here he was, the great pretender, hoodwinked by a smarter puppet master and a woman he thought he'd been gently steering. Manipulated while believing he held the strings. More than once he found himself giving a slow, deliberate clap in the half-lit flat.

"Bravo. Well played."

'Oh what a tangled web we weave, When first we practice to deceive'.

Scott's verse clattered through his skull like loose change. He could still picture the old classroom, smell the chalk dust, feel the quiet rivalry between the handful of lads who took English seriously. He'd once tried to learn the whole of Marmion's final canto with that other bright spark— Dennis something... Dawkins. Yes, that was it. Dandy Dennis Dawkins, the school's proud Oxbridge export, now a silk in some oak-paneled chambers.

A light flickered in Mick's mind. Dawkins owed him. Owed him big. A few years back they'd crossed paths when Mick had been on an entrapment job. Dawkins had breezed up with that lofty confidence he possessed, the kind that turns barristers into courtroom performers.

"Didn't realise you were one of the enlightened, Dorrington, old chap."

"I'm not," Mick had replied, deadpan, "I'm waiting for someone, a woman. But there's a lot of police activity around here today, so I'd be careful if I were you... old chap."

A pointed pause. A mutual understanding, and Dawkins had drifted off, leaving his dignity intact. Later, Mick had simply reported an old schoolmate bumping into him by chance. No mention of the fact that the silk might have been indulging in something less than career friendly.

Now, sitting in the stillness of his suspended life, Mick let the memory settle like dust. Yes...Dawkins owed him. And a QC in full armour was exactly the sort of ally who could stop the powers-that-be 'farting in church', as the old saying went. He finally had a place to begin. Not with anger. Not with heartbreak. But with a measured, deliberate step toward the truth, and maybe, just maybe, a way out of the mess that had swallowed him whole.

Dawkins had been only too willing to step in for his old school-mate. They'd never been close, different circles, different destinies, but that didn't seem to matter now. The moment Mick's name was mentioned, the barrister's eyes had lit with something between curiosity and nostalgia.

"Of course I'll represent him," he'd said, smoothing down his immaculate tie with that theatrical flourish only a seasoned silk could carry off, "Pro bono, naturally." As if he were offering a favour to the boy who once recited Shakespeare in a threadbare school hall, rather than to a disgraced undercover cop whose world had collapsed overnight.

Neither of them knew it then, but something had shifted. What began as a courtesy, a polite nod to a shared past, would harden into something resembling friendship.

And in time, it would become more than that. There would be calls made in quiet corridors, names mentioned in confidence, and courtroom miracles pulled off with the kind of elegance only Dandy Dawkins could muster.

Mick would hand him cases, people in trouble, people who needed a second chance, and Dawkins would ensure they got the very best defence money couldn't buy.

A symbiotic relationship, forged out of necessity, tempered by respect, and built, ironically, on the kind of trust Mick had once believed himself incapable of giving.

In its own strange way, it would become one of the few good things to survive the wreckage of the Harland job. A boost for Dawkins 'ambitions'. And, though Mick would rarely admit it, a lifeline for him.

Mick could only imagine the faces of Porter and his team at Complaints & Discipline when they had received the request for details of any incriminating evidence that was being held on his client, Michael Dorrington.

Jock McAllister had also been sent a similar request. Dawkins knew that they wouldn't release what they had, but that wasn't the point. He merely wanted everyone to know that Mick had a QC in his corner. And it did do the trick, eventually, if not immediately.

Autumn bled into winter, winter thawed into the pale grey of early spring. It was in those first days of Spring 2003 that Mick was summoned to Police Headquarters in Birmingham.

It was Superintendent Porter overseeing things again, but this time it wasn't an interview under caution , no cassette tapes, no sterile preamble. Jock McAllister sat at the table, clutching an A5 folder as if it might try to escape.

Dawkins would later remark that McAllister looked as though he was "absolutely shitting himself," but in the moment Mick only registered the way Jock avoided his eyes, staring instead at the folder like it held his absolution.

Once they'd settled, Porter nodded for the update. He didn't ask Mick, he asked McAllister, which told Mick almost everything he needed to know.

Jock cleared his throat, opened the little folder and began reading, word for word, as though his life depended on sticking to the script.

Victor Harland: Pleaded guilty to seven charges; importation, distribution, laundering. Fifteen years imprisonment.

Tom and Tony O'Dowd: Both pleaded guilty to cocaine distribution and laundering. Twelve years each.

Devlin: Pleaded guilty. Ten years.

Jamie Grant: Not charged. Insufficient evidence to secure a conviction according to the Crown Prosecution Service. That was the first bell. Loud. Sharp. Impossible not to hear.

Michelle O'Grady: Guilty to money laundering. Five years.

Eight other men: assorted guilty pleas, six months to five years.

Jock McAllister's report was conclusive.

Dawkins cut in smoothly, all silk and steel, "Just send full details to Chambers, names, charges, dates, sentences. Everything." Then Mick asked the only question that mattered.

"Was my evidence used at all, sir?"

Porter took over, tone clipped, professional to the point of cruelty.

"Your evidence was not used."

He reached into his briefcase and produced a document as though it were a prize or a threat, it was hard to tell.

"I am also pleased to inform you that the Investigation into your conduct has concluded there is no evidence of criminal wrongdoing."

There was a pause. The sort of pause that loosens the floorboards under your feet. Then came the "but".

"We do, however, have grave concerns regarding your conduct and your ability to understand and follow lawful orders. We also have concerns regarding your physical or mental health."

Mick felt the words settle over him like damp fog; soft, cold, suffocating.

"You will undergo a mandatory medical examination by a

Selected Medical Practitioner. That will determine whether you are fit to continue serving. Until that time, you will remain suspended."

The room felt smaller. Porter closed the file with the finality of a judge's gavel.

Dawkins shifted in his seat.

McAllister stared at his hands.

And Mick simply sat there, quiet, steady, battered in ways he didn't yet have language for. Not guilty. Not needed. Not trusted. Not the same man who'd walked into the operation. Not by a long shot.

That was because he'd been played. Properly played. And now, at last, he could see the shape of it, every hidden hand, every nudge, every lie dressed up as coincidence.

The one element that he hadn't been able to previously figure out was 'why?' Why had Michelle been prepared to allow a man to get close to her, to fall in love with her, only to betray him, but not to save her own skin?

Mick felt that he had now completed the jigsaw.

Somehow, Jock McAllister had caught wind that Michelle O'Grady was Harland's accountant. Maybe an informant had provided the tip, or someone with an axe to grind. She held the keys to Harland's kingdom, could take it apart ledger by ledger if she chose. But she wouldn't. Even staring down a stretch inside, she'd stayed loyal. She wasn't built to be a snitch. Threaten her with prison? Useless. Threaten her with Harland's wrath? Even less effective. Harland didn't warn people, he made examples. But her sister's husband, Jamie? That was different.

The thought of Jamie banged up for probably years, her sister's home gutted of its centre... that would have broken her. The twins bewildered, without their father, her beloved sister inconsolable without her husband. That would make Michelle reconsider. That would make her look for a way to shield the people she loved.

So, she'd agreed, quietly, miserably, to make sure the evidence was exactly where the police needed it when the raids came. Make sure Harland's empire had a weak point. Make sure the sums didn't balance just enough. But Jamie had to walk; that was the price she demanded for her disloyalty.

Except she couldn't do it outright. Harland would never forgive her. He'd sniff it out eventually, and then her life wouldn't be worth the price of a pint.

So, Jock had found the solution. A distraction. A fall guy. A patsy. Someone to take the heat of Michelle. Forever.

And guess who that was? The penny didn't just drop. It plummeted.

Michelle had never screamed when the door went in. She'd given him that odd, sad smile, as if apologising for something she couldn't say out loud.

Jock had lied to his face about the Investigation. The drugs, the money, the ledgers, none of it had mattered in the end. They'd never needed Mick's evidence at all. They knew they'd already secured the evidence needed. They'd get their conviction. They'd seize every penny of his assets. They just needed Harland to blame someone, anyone, other than Michelle when he went hunting for the traitor in his organisation. The seeds had probably been sown in the days before the raids: a quiet whisper from a 'bent cop', a hint of a hint, just enough to suggest that someone close to Harland had bumped their gums to the police. No names, of course. Just a rumour about some out-of-towner who'd been getting a little too cosy with the wrong people.

And Mick, poor, blind, self-assured Mick, had marched straight through the middle of their perfect little setup, convinced he was calling the tune, when all the while he'd been moving to theirs. A patsy with a pulse. A ready-made explanation for Harland when the walls came down. A distraction so neat and so expendable that Jock must have toasted himself the moment the trap snapped shut.

And Michelle? She'd gotten what she wanted. Okay, she would do a few years inside, but her sister's family would never have to suffer disruption or shame.

In the end, Mick realised, he hadn't infiltrated their world at all. He'd merely played the part they'd written for him.

~

IT TOOK a fortnight for the letter to land on Mick's doormat, but once it did, he had a whole month to stew over it. A thick white envelope containing forms, instructions, and the unmistakable reek of bureaucratic judgement dressed up as pastoral concern.

The Initial Wellbeing Questionnaire came first, pages of questions about his childhood, his family, the bruises and joys of growing up, then his adult life, relationships, losses, secrets, nightmares. He was to dredge through all of it, lay himself bare for people who didn't know him and probably didn't care. A life autopsy written in biro.

Another form demanded his signature so his local doctor could release every scrap of medical history he had. Every flu jab, every fracture, every prescription. They wanted all of him neatly catalogued.

Then the main event: a mandatory two-day evaluation at a private clinic in Birmingham. A 'Specialist Assessment'. Somewhere glossy and discreet, full of leather chairs and low voices. Somewhere designed to put men like him under a microscope. At the bottom of the letter, in bold and full of reassurance that only made it worse:

'This Medical Assessment is NOT a punitive measure. It is NOT part of a disciplinary process. It is an in-depth evaluation to assess your fitness, including your psychological stability for the role of Police Officer. It will determine your fitness for duty, considering your mental and emotional stability over time. The process is CONFIDENTIAL'.

The final page named the Selected Medical Practitioner: Dr David Buchanan, with a clinical psychologist, Dr Sarah Williams, assisting. Two strangers, professionals undoubtedly, selected to make a decision that would change the rest of his life.

Mick had to sign a declaration that he would be willing to attend the medical evaluation which would take place on 1st and 2nd of September 2003.

~

EVERYONE at the West Midlands Area Private Health Assessment Centre in Edgbaston treated Mick with the sort of warmth usually reserved for private clients who pay in crisp banknotes. Respectful smiles, gentle voices, polished manners, the whole performance. It was a professional outfit, no question about that. The receptionists, nurses, porters, every one of them immaculate in matching claret-and-blue uniforms, all bright eyes and clipped tones. Mick couldn't help wondering whether someone in recruitment had been tasked with hiring only the young, the photogenic and the untroubled. A corporate image to soothe the soul, or distract it.

He arrived a few minutes before his 10.0 a.m. appointment. The receptionist asked him to sign the register and jot down his vehicle details for 'security purposes', her pen already poised before he'd finished speaking. Then she asked him to take a seat. He'd barely touched the cushion before her phone rang. Thirty seconds later she was ushering him toward Room A with a practiced smile. Efficient; too efficient. Like they'd been waiting for him to enter stage left on cue.

Room A was clinically pleasant: pale green walls, a round table set with a jug of water, four tumblers arranged as if expecting company that never arrived. No artwork, no notices, nothing to catch the eye. A room designed for focus, or confession.

Dr David Buchanan was already seated, late forties, neat grey hair, trimmed grey beard. Blue slacks, blue blazer, pale shirt open at the collar.

He had the glow of a man who'd just stepped out of a squash court or a sauna, refreshed, relaxed, perfectly centred.

Beside him sat Dr Sarah Williams. Early forties, slim, auburn hair pinned neatly in a bun, dressed sharply in a pencil skirt and white blouse. Bookish, but with an unexpected softness about her. The sort who smiled kindly as she handed you the shovel you were expected to bury yourself with.

Later, Mick would always reflect on them as, 'The Doctors of Doom', but for now, he just needed to sit and listen.

Mick did as instructed and took a seat. Buchanan opened with the familiar spiel, try to relax, be open and honest, no right or wrong answers, stop us if anything needs clarification. All the lines rehearsed to sound reassuring, yet they carried a faint echo of inevitability. Mick felt a prickle at the back of his neck. These people didn't strike him as the sort who arrived at a room without already knowing the ending.

Then Buchanan opened Mick's questionnaire and began reading through it, every line, every answer, word for bloody word. Occasionally he paused, asking Mick to confirm that what he'd written was accurate. Sometimes Dr Williams leaned in with a carefully phrased follow-up, her tone gentle, her eyes too attentive.

It didn't take a detective to spot where their interests lay. They lingered on certain sections longer than others; Mick could almost see the bold headings in their minds. They weren't exploring. They were excavating.

The first area they dug into was his relationship with his father. That didn't surprise him. It was always fathers, mothers or childhood ghosts with these people. But the way they went at it, with soft questions wrapped around steel hooks, felt like they weren't looking for clarity. They were looking for confirmation. And Mick couldn't shake the feeling that whatever judgement this pair would eventually write, the ink was already dry.

An hour slid by before Buchanan finally leaned back, tapping his fingers together like a man pleased with the neatness of his own handiwork. He spoke in that slow, practiced voice of his, warm, sympathetic, and utterly clinical.

"You describe your father," he began, "As having rather... Victorian values. Rigid with your mother, rigid with you. And because those values conflicted with your own, tension was inevitable. You were never as close to him as you were to your mother. I'm not suggesting you didn't love him, Mick, but it seems you didn't particularly like him, and knowing that must have been painful."

He paused, letting the words settle, like silt drifting through water, "So you learned to run. Not only away from home that day when you were eight, but away from yourself. You hid in books, in plays, drama as a metaphorical escape from your own skin. Roles, characters, masks. A pattern you later... repeated, shall we say, in your police career."

Dr Williams nodded softly, her pen making those delicate, deliberate scratches that Mick was becoming uncomfortably aware of. Notes. Interpretations. Judgements. He wasn't sure which.

Buchanan continued, "And when your father's mind began to fail, his memory fading,...when at times he didn't know who you were... oddly, that's when you felt closest to him. Because you no longer had to play the part of a 'son'. There were no expectations. No history. You were finally free to care for him without the weight of what had come before. You couldn't disappoint him, because he had no expectations of you."

Mick felt something tighten behind his ribs; not quite anger, not quite fear, but something close to both. They were painting his life with confident strokes, as though he were a case study they knew by heart. As though he were confirming a theory they'd agreed on over morning coffee. He didn't contradict them. Didn't trust himself to. But he felt flayed open all the same.

Yes, he hadn't liked his father. Yes, the dementia had made the old man easier to love. But hearing it dissected, labelled, boxed, it felt clinical, pre-ordained, as if they were arranging evidence for a verdict they'd already decided upon.

The narrative continued—his school days, his early police service, the ease with which he'd learned to slip between identities. Sometimes agreeing to take on roles even though he fundamentally disagreed with there aims, such as the early vice work he had undertaken. Buchanan spoke as though Mick had been rehearsing his whole life for undercover work, because that was how he could escape from himself, as though every choice he'd made was a footnote to some deeper psychological flaw.

Mick listened, face impassive, but a cold certainty began creeping into him. This wasn't an assessment. This was a diagnosis waiting for a signature. And he was the only one in the room who didn't yet know what he'd been diagnosed with.

Dr Williams tapped her pencil against her full, immaculately glossed lips, watching him with that soft, professional curiosity that never quite reached her eyes.

"It seems," she said gently, "That adopting roles hasn't only been a professional necessity for you, Mick. It's been... a refuge."

Buchanan nodded, taking the thread. "You didn't just play undercover roles," he said, "You inhabited them. Micky Dee. Micky Robinson. Mikey Vaughan. These weren't disguises, they were lives. You describe each of them with an ease, a fluency that's almost absent when you talk about being simply... Mick Dorrington."

Dr Buchanan let the silence settle for a moment, then moved his glasses a fraction further up the bridge of his nose, as though adjusting focus on the man across the table.

"Let's explore something you've been hinting at Mr. Dorrington. You've described, sometimes directly and sometimes hinted, that living as someone else has always felt easier than living as yourself. That's not uncommon in this line of work, but with you it seems... more than occupational necessity."

He glanced at Dr Williams, who gave a small, encouraging nod, her pencil poised.

"Micky Robinson. Micky Dee. Mikey Vaughan. Each identity carefully constructed, each with its own emotional tone, its own history, its own moral tolerances. And yet when we trace your most significant attachments, your most passionate decisions, even your most reckless impulses... they don't belong to Mick Dorrington at all. They belong to your aliases." He spoke without malice, almost gently.

"Your marriage to Bernadette, for instance. You speak of it as Mick, dutiful, hopeful, occasionally distracted. But when we compare your emotional responses, the intensity, the longing, the vulnerability you showed with Michelle O'Grady... those weren't the feelings of Mick Dorrington. They were the feelings of Mikey Vaughan. A man who didn't technically exist."

Dr Williams folded her hands lightly. "It isn't that you didn't love Bernie," she added softly. "But Mick loved Bernie in a way that was... muted. Safe. Familiar. But Mikey—Mikey loved Michelle with a fire that seems alien to the rest of your life. Fire can warm, but it can also burn. And in that case, it nearly consumed you."

They let that sit.

Buchanan leaned back slightly, as though giving Mick room to breathe.

"This is important because it shows something crucial. When you step into an identity, you do not simply use it, the way most undercover operatives do. You inhabit it. You surrender judgment to it. The role doesn't free you—it governs you."

His voice stayed calm, but the subtext had sharpened, "And that creates risk, serious risk. Because Mick Dorrington understands policing ethics. Mick knows the law, knows the boundaries, knows why they matter. But your aliases... they don't. They operate by their own rules, the rules that make sense inside the world you've built for them."

A quiet beat and Dr Williams spoke first this time, her tone embroidered with sympathy yet aimed like a scalpel. She continued, "Which brings us to Michelle. You knew, as Mick, that entering a sexual relationship while undercover wasn't permitted. You knew it was unethical. You also knew it was, strictly speaking, criminal. But Mikey did it anyway. You justified it as operational necessity at first, but you've since acknowledged there were personal motives... deeper motives."

Buchanan leaned in. "And that is the concern, Mr. Dorrington. The line between necessity and desire blurred. Your judgment changed. The alias began making decisions that Mick never would have. Decisions that risked an operation, risked an innocent woman, and risked yourself."

His fingers tapped once, slowly, on the table, "Undercover policing requires flexibility, but not moral drift. And what we see here is something more dangerous; your ability to submerge so fully into an identity that you stop evaluating consequences through your own moral framework. You become, in effect, a law unto yourself. Not out of malice. Out of immersion. Out of escape." He paused, "Out of need."

Dr Williams closed her notebook gently. "And that, in combination with the emotional entanglements, the secrecy, the decisions made in character rather than in conscience... that tells us not that you are a bad man, Mr. Dorrington, but that the work has reshaped you so profoundly that the boundaries between duty and performance have eroded." Then, quietly, "And that erosion, however heroic its intentions, can be catastrophic."

Buchanan tapped his wristwatch, "I think now would be a good time for a break for lunch. Back in forty-five minutes, is that okay?"

Mick didn't feel like eating. He sat in his car listening to his thoughts. They darted around in his head like a firecracker, ignited and placed in a biscuit tin. It was a symptom of being in a scenario that he could not manipulate. He was not calling the shots.

After lunch the assessment continued in a similar vein. Dr Buchanan folded his hands, the picture of patient academic concern, but his eyes had sharpened. Mick recognised the shift. He'd seen the look before, in informants, in villains, in senior officers pretending to be reasonable just before the trap snapped shut.

"Let's now turn," Buchanan said gently, "To your work practices." Mick nodded cautiously.

"You have, over the years, engineered operational conditions that allowed you to work alone, sometimes entirely unsupervised. You've insisted on controlling the pace, the direction, and the operational parameters. You've consistently argued that it was necessary, operationally necessary, because only you understood the risks."

"That's right," Mick replied, keeping his tone level, "Most senior officers will openly admit that they don't know the first thing about working undercover. They rely on my experience. They'll ask how we are going to conduct the operation. If they were to set the pace, the operation could be jeopardised. Maybe someone dies. A source, an access agent...., me."

Dr Sarah Williams leaned forward, her voice soft but scalpel precise, "But you must see how that sounds, Mick. You present your approach as pragmatic, but what we hear is something more...selfreferential. A conviction that only you can do it correctly. That others, your supervisors, your command chain, are, to put it bluntly, liabilities."

"I never said they were idiots. They have just never done undercover work, and many have never run covert operations, or they are very inexperienced. They need my experience. They ask for my experience. Are they wrong to seek my advice?" Mick said sharply.

"No," Buchanan agreed, "But the implication hangs heavy in everything you've described. You don't trust them. You use their inexperience to circumvent them, to usurp them. You manipulate scenarios so that they can't interfere."

Mick opened his mouth, but Buchanan continued.

"We've read the reports of previous ops. When you insisted on operating without a cover team. When you refused surveillance. When you demanded complete anonymity even from your own side. You framed it as operational protection." He paused before continuing, "But it granted you absolute freedom. No oversight. No corrective mechanism. No boundary."

Sarah added, "Do you see how that can be interpreted? Particularly alongside your pattern of immersing yourself into identities with emotional intensity. Micky Dee, Mickey Robinson, Mikey Vaughan...each allowed you to operate outside ordinary constraints. Each identity came equipped with its own moral code, convenient to the situation."

"That's part of the job," Mick said, "You take on a role. You become what the criminals expect to see."

"Up to a point," Sarah replied softly. "But the evidence suggests you don't merely 'take on' a role. You live it. You invest in it. You give it emotional territory that should belong only to Mick Dorrington. Your decision to engage sexually with Miss O'Grady, knowing it breached every rule in the book, wasn't made by Mick. It was made by Mikey."

The second time that had been brought up.

She continued, "You've admitted that you knew it was prohibited. You knew it could destroy prosecutions, damage public trust, ruin your career. Yet you proceeded. You justified it as necessary for the operation— but the truth is that it satisfied something in you, Mick.

Something emotional. Something central to how you survive under-cover environments."

"Look, the truth is that I was told to do it by Jock McAllister, the Officer in Charge of the Operation."

"So", Sarah continued, "Just supposing for a moment, that it was true Detective Superintendent McAllister told you to engage in a sexual relationship with Miss O'Grady, would this be one of the few times that you have actually trusted a senior officer enough to follow their guidance, rather than using your own experience and knowledge to have followed the right path?"

Mick stared at the water jug. His own reflection trembled in the curve of the glass. Buchanan's voice cut in, steady, clinical.

"That's the danger, you see. In character, you will do things that Mick would find morally abhorrent. Illegal. Reckless. Self-destructive. You rationalise it afterwards as operational necessity, but the deeper truth is simpler, the identity takes over. It allows behaviours you would never permit under your true name."

Mick exhaled slowly. "I did what I was told to do - what I had to do."

"But that isn't quite true is it? The senior officer was never aware of your intention of becoming sexually involved with an individual who was a subject of the operation. And that," Buchanan added, "Is precisely the problem. Not what you did, Mick. But that you alone decided what had to be done. You set the rules. You broke them. You justified the breaking. Again and again.

Sarah's voice followed, quiet but final.

"You've become a man who does not follow rules when he believes those rules are wrong. A man who manipulates operational parameters to grant himself independence. A man whose judgement can be commandeered by the very roles he creates. That is not a criticism of your courage or your ability. It is an assessment of risk."

They Both looked at him with a strange mixture of pity and respect—like surgeons studying a patient with a tumour no one had spotted growing.

Buchanan concluded, almost kindly: "And it is why we must

determine whether Mick Dorrington, the man, not the role, is still capable of serving as a police officer within a lawful structure. Because right now, everything suggests you have become a law unto yourself." Again he paused before continuing, "And that I think will be enough for today. We both thank you for your honesty with us. Tomorrow, I would like to explore some of the threats and dangers you have faced while working undercover, and then I hope to be able to run through some hypothetical scenarios with you, to see how you would deal with or react to a developing threat."

As Mick drove away from the centre all he could hear were the words of Dr Buchanan.

"The senior officer was never aware of your intention of becoming sexually involved with an individual who was a subject of the operation."

THE FOLLOWING DAY, same room, same stale water jug, same two faces pretending neutrality, except Mick walked in knowing the verdict was already inked somewhere in a file he'd never read. This wasn't about saving a career anymore. It was about leaving with whatever scraps of dignity he still owned. Pride was a thin shield, but it was all he had left.

Buchanan didn't waste time.

"Tell me, Mick, how many times have you been in imminent danger? Times when you genuinely feared for your life."

Mick let the silence breathe. He tapped his fingers on the table, one after the other, like a kid counting out punishment lines. Ninety seconds passed before he finally lifted his gaze.

"Never."

Buchanan blinked, thrown off just enough to show it.

"Never? The reports of bravery, commendations, witness accounts —they all say otherwise. You've been inches from death more times than we can count."

Mick gave a slow shrug and then responded, "You said it yourself yesterday, that wasn't me. Not really. That was Micky. Or Mikey. Or whatever name I was wearing that week. Those lads don't get to be afraid. Fear's a luxury they can't afford. You let even a flicker show, and you're done. Jobs collapse. People get hurt. Sometimes people die."

He leaned back, eyes steady, voice low but sharp enough to nick glass.

"So no. I have never feared anything. Because I don't have to. They're the ones you read about. They can take the risks."

Across the table, Buchanan and Sarah Williams scribbled as though racing to keep up, pens scratching like small accusations. Trying to capture him. Trying to pin him to the page.

Mick kept his face unreadable, but inside he felt the slow grind of something giving way, pride, patience, the last threads of the life he once recognised.

Buchanan leaned back, fingers steepled, the faintest hint of academic triumph in his eyes, as though Mick had just confirmed a theory he'd been nursing for months.

"So," the doctor said softly, "when the danger came, it wasn't you in the firing line at all. It was one of your creations. One of your... masks."

He spoke slowly, carefully, choosing each word like stepping stones across a river with no visible bottom.

"That's right. The fear belongs to them. Not me."

"And because they can take risks," Sarah cut in, "You can avoid feeling anything at all. Responsibility. Doubt. Consequences." Her tone was mild, clinical even, but something in it prickled Mick's skin. It felt too prepared. Too rehearsed. Like she was guiding him toward a conclusion already written in their notes.

"I did what was required to do the job that I had been asked to do," he replied evenly. "Nothing more."

Buchanan tilted his head. "But that's the point, isn't it? When you become Micky, or Mikey, or whoever the job needs, the usual rules no longer apply. Not your rules. And certainly not the Police Service's rules."

"That's bullshit," Mick snapped, quicker, sharper than intended.

Both doctors registered it, like crows spotting a glint in a field.

"In undercover work," Mick continued, controlling his breathing, "You operate differently because you must. Senior officers don't understand that. They never have. That's why I've always insisted on doing things my way...because it works. It got results. It took down people they couldn't touch. It protected sources, it kept them alive. It kept me alive."

Sarah exchanged a look with Buchanan. It was brief but not brief enough. A look that said, 'there it is'.

Buchanan uncapped his pen, voice low and deliberate. "Mr. Dorrington... can you see how that sounds? You dictate the terms. You choose the methods. You dismiss oversight because you think you know better. You justify breaking rules because you believe the mission depends on your judgement alone."

"I followed the rules that kept me alive," he repeated, quieter this time. "And that kept others alive."

"Others?" Buchanan prompted gently.

He had walked into a trap. He felt it now. They weren't assessing him. They were confirming what they had already decided.

Tell us about a time you disagreed with a manager on covert tactics.

Which year? Which manager? Take your pick.

What crimes would you be prepared to commit to maintain cover?

The one question no sane undercover officer answers honestly.

Actually, the one question that no sane undercover officer can answer honestly, because they just don't know. In an infinite number of scenarios, there are an infinite number of reasons for maintaining cover.

So, Mick gave them the polished answers. The safe ones. The rehearsed ones. He wasn't about to hand them the rope they were already itching to watch him hang from.

"That's what concerns us," Sarah said, leaning forward, her voice soft but implacable. "In character, you become someone who doesn't just bend rules, he abandons them. Someone who sleeps with an operation target. Someone who is willing to commit offences because he thinks the ends justify the means. Someone who believes that only he can see the bigger picture."

Mick felt his pulse in his throat. He wanted to argue, God, he wanted to, but the words wouldn't come. Not because they were wrong, but because they were turning the truth inside out. Using pieces of him to build a version he barely recognised.

Buchanan set his pen down with the kind of deliberate care that told Mick the next line had already been scripted.

"We need a forty-five-minute break. I've phone calls to make. Shall we take lunch now and resume afterwards?"

Lunch. Mick couldn't imagine anything less appetising. He wasn't hungry. Right now, he was a cocktail of anger, frustration, weariness and something that felt a lot like grief. But he nodded, because nodding was easier than caring.

When they returned, the mood in the room had shifted. The air felt heavier, as if the walls themselves had decided the verdict and were just humouring the performance. Buchanan and Williams took turns firing questions, soft-voiced, clinical, predictable, each one designed to lure him toward some pre-chosen diagnosis.

The first question was pitched like a friendly lob. Sarah leaned forward.

"Have you ever been asked for your name, and had to stop and think which identity you were at that moment? Whether you were Mick, Micky, Mikey... or someone else?"

Mick frowned. "No. Of course not."

A faint, almost pitying smile crossed her face. "That's interesting, because your medical records show some confusion when a paramedic asked your name in 1991. You'd had an accident..."

"A bike accident," Mick cut in, "I was concussed. Anyone would be confused. It wasn't because I forgot which character I was playing."

Unruffled, she checked her notes. "And you had a brain scan..."

"Every part of me was scanned," Mick said, "Head to toe. Nothing wrong."

She lifted her eyes. "Were you ever told the result of the brain scan?"

He couldn't resist the jab. "They couldn't find anything." A beat. "I mean wrong. Couldn't find anything wrong."

Despite herself, Sarah's mouth twitched, almost a smile. Buchanan shut it down with a curt, "Right, Doctor Williams, let's move on."

And they did, straight into the competency theatre. Scenarios he'd been fed a dozen times over the years, except this time they weren't tests; they were ammunition. They wanted reactions they could file under Unmanageable. Risk-prone. Rogue. Each question felt like another push toward the conclusion they'd already underlined.

Describe a time you solved an operational problem with limited resources.

Pick one of a hundred.

And so it went on until finally, with a grave little nod, Buchanan closed his folder.

"Do you have any questions for us?"

Mick considered the room, the pale green walls, the jug of untouched water, the two faces pretending to be impartial, and decided he had just one thing left he could say without losing himself.

"Yes," he said calmly, "Is Detective Superintendent Jock McAllister having one of these assessments too? Because he is one slimy, devious, sick-in-the-head bastard who really does need psycho-analysis." He paused momentarily, "And please, quote me word for word on that."

WEST MIDLANDS POLICE sent copies of the Selected Medical Practitioner's Health Assessment to both Mick and to Dawkins. The report was dated 9th September 2003. Just a week to compile. Either very efficient or pre-determined. Mick had his theory.

After a lot of introductory blurb about place, time etc., of the assessment and those conducting it, the text provided the findings as follows:

Major Psychological and Mental Health Issues Evident:

Burnout: Intense, prolonged job stress, in high threat environments leading to emotional exhaustion, cynicism and reduced effectiveness affecting performance;

Depression and anxiety: High prevalence of stress, low mood, anxiety and significant mental health problems linked to work;

Impaired Judgement and Emotional Dis-regulation: Difficulty managing emotional responses, increased irritability, heightened aggression and changes in perception, including loss of trust.

Contributing Organisational Factors: Workload and work-life balance: Excessive demands, stressful working environments, cancelled rest and leave days, and chronic fatigue;

Signs of Unfitness for Duty: Significant mood swings, irritability and depression. Social withdrawal, loss of interest in family life and hobbies.

Changes in behaviour, conflict with senior officers, inability to follow lawful orders and abide by police regulations or inability to adhere to own personal values, blurred lines between legal activity and lawbreaking;

Recklessness and thrill seeking, deliberately seeking out dangerous scenarios, failing to recognise the threat to his own personal safety or operational effectiveness, feeling of invincibility, believes his own risk evaluation is better than senior officers;

Potential Dissociative Identity Disorder (with no evidence of childhood abuse), increasing examples of uncertainty of identity, blurring lines between actual and adopted identities, and assuming behavioural standards of an adopted identity;

Inability to follow orders, no longer trusts senior officers and will ignore a lawful order or take action that opposes a lawful order.

Further examination required:

- Existing medical evidence of brain scan may reveal indication of some minor damage to the Amygdala, potentially impairing ability to recognise fear in self and emotions in others. This is a very rare condition and further exploration may be required. The ability to recognise fear is a crucial factor in evaluating the safety of self or others.

***

As he read through the assessment, he had no delusions of what was being said about him in polite medical speak. Years moving through shadows on borrowed names had taken its toll. On paper they called it 'occupational burnout', the kind bred from too many threats, too little sleep, and a career spent pretending to be someone who couldn't afford to blink. In plain English: the job had hollowed him out.

They had painted him as a man whose patience had frayed to the wire, irritable, unpredictable, suspicious. A copper who no longer trusted the sound of his own heartbeat.

They noted 'changes in perception'; 'difficulty managing emotions'; 'loss of trust.' He noted that they made it sound awfully poetic for a slow-motion breakdown and he almost laughed when he read the section about contributing organisational factors. It was like listing the rain as a contributing factor to a flood. 'No shit, Sherlock!'

Where the knife twisted were the indications of unfitness to do the job. They should have just written, ' Mick Dorrington had stopped playing by the Queen's rules'.

'Failing to recognise threats'? He wondered who the hell they thought they'd been sending undercover all those years, an accountant? 'Difficulty differentiating between legal actions and criminal mimicry." Or, to put it another way, Mick had lived in the grey so long he'd forgotten the black and white.

'Potential Dissociative Identity Disorder!' They slid this across the table as though it were a quiet suggestion, not an accusation.

'Identity confusion... blurring between adopted personas...

assuming the emotional responses of false identities...' To Mick, it felt like they were saying he'd misplaced himself somewhere between Mick, Micky, and Mikey, and wasn't quite sure how to get back. And the kicker: 'No childhood abuse present.' Meaning the disorder, if it existed, had been grown in the soil of the job, not his past.

'Failure to follow lawful orders'. This they delivered with almost smug certainty. A man who would follow a plan, but only if he wrote it. A man who trusted his instincts more than the brass. A man who would improvise because he believed he was the only one capable of pulling the strings properly. They called it personality drift. He called it survival. Same facts, different stories.

And then came the final quiet blow...Further Examination Required. 'Possible neurological impairment'. Old brain scan indicating minor damage to the amygdala. If true, it might explain why fear rarely visited him. In undercover work, that's useful... In real life, it's a warning sign. A sign that he had been unaware had existed in himself.

He remained unaware that it had also existed in one, Victor Harland.

Within 7-days the letter arrived, thin, official, and final in the way only police authority stationery can be. West Midlands Police Authority, in its politely strangled prose, informed him that 'On the advice of the Selected Medical Practitioner, he was deemed no longer fit to undertake ordinary police duties'.

Just like that. Twenty years of graft, danger, near-deaths, and shadows, reduced to a recommendation from the 'doctors of doom', who had already looked at him as though the verdict had been written long before Mick opened his mouth.

They were generous enough to add that he would still be 'fit for employment in other non-police work', which read like a joke delivered with a straight face. What other work did they imagine? Undercover police officers don't go into retail.

He was to be retired on a Lower-Tier Ill-Health Pension. Lower-tier, of course. The bottom shelf. A polite way of saying. 'broken, but not broken enough to cost us real money'.

His twenty years bought him a taxfree lump sum, six thousand pounds, barely enough to buy off a few ghosts, and twelve grand a year, padded slightly by an ill-health enhancement that felt more like hush money than gratitude.

His official last day in the job was stamped out in neat black ink: 05 October 2003. A sentence more than a date.

They hadn't fired him. That would imply he'd done something wrong. They hadn't honoured him. That would imply he'd done something right. Instead, they'd taken the middle road, the one that leaves a man standing on the pavement with nothing but a formal letter in his hand and the faint sense that he had been quietly erased.

Mick folded the letter and placed it back into the envelope, as though shutting it away might somehow undo everything. But it stayed there on the table, pale as a death certificate, reminding him that the system had finally done what a dozen near-misses, a handful of bullets, and Victor Harland never managed. It retired him.

And for the first time in his life, Mick Dorrington wasn't sure who he was supposed to be next.

15

LIFE AFTER LIFE

"We'll appeal. Sue their fucking serge-covered fat arses for every penny we can. It's complete and utter bollocks. Who are these so-called experts." Dawkins was animated. Not faux animated like when he was literally performing in court. No, genuinely fuming.

It was in that moment Mick knew, absolutely, finally, that he and Dawkins would be tied together for life. The barrister cared. Even a man who'd spent half his adult years pretending to feel things could see that.

"I appreciate it, truly," Mick said, rubbing a thumb over the spine of the suspension papers. "But no. I'm not appealing. We might win, and then what? I'm back wearing a uniform, doing something utterly mindcrushing for the next ten years; guarding a litter bin the Chief Constable's particularly fond of... school-crossing liaison... Officer-in-Charge of lightbulbs. They'd bury me in pettiness until I threw my own ticket in. No. No appeal. No suing them either. I need to keep at least some dignity intact."

Dawkins frowned. Genuine concern softened his otherwise polished features.

"And what then, old chap? What do you plan on doing?"

Mick let out a breath somewhere between a sigh and a laugh.

"The last twenty-odd years have left me with... talents. Someone, somewhere, will have use for them. I've got a half-decent pension, I only need to top it up. Worst case scenario, I'll get myself a paper round." He grinned, though it didn't reach his eyes.

Dawkins studied him for a moment, fingers steepled, the way expensive lawyers do when they're weighing up a human being like a promising brief.

"Hmm. You do have talents, remarkable talents, if I may say so. Talents I might, on occasion, need to call upon." He paused, letting the line hang between them like bait, "For example..." And then came the case. An arson in Evesham. Estranged wife's house torched to cinders. Petrol-soaked gloves in the client's garage.

A witness claiming they'd seen the husband legging it from the scene.

"All very damning," Dawkins said lightly, "Except my client swears blind he didn't do it. And, I'll admit, my instincts say he's being framed. This is where you come in, Mick, old boy."

The story continued to unravel; the client was a biker, a 'hangabout' according to Dawkins, but Mick knew what he meant, riding with some up-and-coming club in Gloucestershire. Had annoyed the wrong man by taking his old lady to bed. Now she'd vanished, and the client reckoned it was because she knew too much about the set-up, and was scared witless.

"I wondered," Dawkins continued, "If a man familiar with the biker world could... make enquiries. Quietly. Discreetly. See if the young lady might be found, and might help us in court. You wouldn't happen to know anyone who could do such work, for a favourable hourly rate and expenses covered?"

Of course Mick knew someone. Himself.

It was the first of many cases he'd take on for Dawkins, and later, for half the legal profession in the Midlands. Word travelled fast: when a barrister needed someone found, someone shadowed, someone checked out... Mick Dorrington was the man you called.

Not everything was crime. He took the private jobs too: missing kids, cheating spouses, runaways, lost goods, the little tragedies and petty betrayals that kept the world turning.

A few big consumer brands hired him quietly, wanting proof that some market-stall chancer was shifting knocked-off designer goods that looked like theirs. And now and again, he'd stand shoulder-to-shoulder with some nervous visiting foreign businessman convinced Birmingham was full of muggers, kidnappers and assassins. Easy money.

He didn't have the institutional backup anymore, but over time he would rebuild a toolkit of fake IDs, burner phones, and carefully curated contacts. He even resurrected Micky Dee, the alias nobody would ever link to the supposedly dead biker. And some of the old friends, cops, the good ones, still helped where they could. A quiet PNC check. A Vehicle Registration Number lookup, which gave the name and address of a vehicle owner. A name run through a system. Nobody ever asked him for favours back. They did it because they new that if Mick needed those details, it was for a good cause, not a bad one.

And that old streak of luck, the one he always swore was his real superpower, never left him. So many times he recalled complimentary responses when he claimed to be lucky. "Ah, but you make your own luck, Mick," people would often say, which he believed showed a complete ignorance of the concept of luck.

He believed that luck was a phenomenon or belief that success or failure, positive or negative results, were sometimes, maybe only occasionally, but sometimes entirely brought about by chance, rather than by any influential actions. Therefore, the ability to 'make your own luck' is an impossibility, if you bring about your own success, that's a skill, not luck.

Two weeks after Dawkins had slid the file across the desk, Mick presented him with a handwritten witness statement from one Miss Lucy Tobin, better known in certain biking circles as 'Mistletoe'. A biker girl who'd been there, who'd seen the set-up, who was ready to testify because she wanted out. Full name. Contact details. Everything tied with a bow.

Dawkins stared at him as if he'd just watched a man pull a rabbit out of a hat.

"How the fuck did you do that so quickly? You're a magician."

"Just luck, old boy," Mick said, the barest hint of a smirk tugging at his mouth, and it wasn't even a lie. He'd found the club's new haunt. Spotted an old Vagabonds Motor Cycle face who clearly hadn't heard the rumour that Mick was supposed to be dead. A few boozy nights later he had the lead he needed, the old club photo, the whisper of a direction to look. The rest was legwork, and the soft-voiced, steady-eyed approach that stopped 'Mistletoe' from screaming or pepper-spraying him when he finally knocked on her door.

And that was that. Case saved. Client freed. Dawkins impressed. And Mick's second life, his real life now, had quietly, irresistibly begun.

A week or so later, as a reward for his help, Dawkins had treated Mick to a slap-up meal at his favourite restaurant in town. They had chatted amiably all night, Dawkins being his usual animated self. They laughed, frowned, cried together, as best friends do. When Dawkins overheard someone making a derogatory, clearly homo-phobic comment about 'their sorts getting everywhere', which Mick had found particularly amusing, he had suggested that it was about time that Mick should find a good woman to love and look after him, as he grew older.

"Oh no, I've done with women, old chap."

"Ooh, so there's a chance for me yet then?" Mick didn't need to respond.

Later, he would drift back to thoughts of Bernie and Michelle, the two women he had ever truly loved. One he'd failed, the other had almost certainly failed him. Still, he found himself muttering, almost defensively, "She had her reasons... she had some mitigation."

The bitterness that had once burned hot had thinned to some-thing duller, something closer to resignation. Time had a way of sanding the edges off even the deepest wounds. But one resolve stayed sharp: he wasn't built for love. Not the ordinary kind, not the kind that grows roots. Whatever wiring a man needed to keep a relationship alive, he didn't have it. Not anymore. Maybe never.

Very occasionally, dark nights, quiet ones, even before his fate had been sealed by the two 'doctors of doom', he had occasionally sought out the company of women of the night. Toms, whores, working girls, call them what you like. Mick had always thought the slang said more about the men who used it than the women themselves.

He respected them, oddly enough. They weren't asking for promises he couldn't keep. They didn't want a version of him he couldn't maintain. They didn't expect Mick Dorrington, or Micky Dee, or any other bloody alias. They just wanted the money on the night, and he wanted the silence afterward.

He was never the sort to treat anyone like a commodity. He paid his fee like any other client, but he'd bring small offerings, flowers, good chocolates, sometimes a bottle of something fizzy. Not as payment; as courtesy. As a reminder that he still had some softness left, tucked away where the job hadn't quite choked it out.

Over time, he became a familiar face to one particular girl, Tissy. She'd done glamour modelling once and had been on her way to making something of it, until a drunk with a Stanley knife carved that future right out of her skin. A slash across the face, more across her torso. All because she'd told him to sod off. The camera gigs dried up. But she still had a body men would pay for, and she still had a stubborn sort of pride. She didn't want pity. She wanted clients who didn't flinch.

Mick never flinched. He never asked questions, and she liked that about him. Two broken souls sharing borrowed time, nothing asked, nothing owed. For a man who lived most of his life wearing other men's faces, that kind of honesty was the closest thing to peace Mick had found in years. So, when she needed a favour, something real, something dangerous , there was only one name she dared speak... Mick's.

Tissy had never used a pimp; she'd always kept her own counsel, skimmed her own earnings. She was choosy with clients, too. Truth be told, she wouldn't have gone near Mick at first glance, he had the look of a man who might turn unpredictable if the night tilted the wrong way. But the other girls said he was different: polite, sober, respectful. One even said she'd genuinely enjoyed her hour with him. That was rare. Very rare. So Tissy took a punt on him, on Mick the punter. She never regretted it.

The trouble came in the form of Paul Dale, an oily, ageing tyrant with delusions of empire and a business card he liked to wave like a royal decree. He wanted Tissy for his escort outfit. Told her it would be 'in her best interests'. Didn't take no for an answer. A woman with her looks could earn him a fortune. He had clients with very specific tastes.

When Mick heard her plea, he told her he'd, "Reason with the bloke, man to man."

Tissy knew better than to argue.

That was when Paul Dale first heard the name Micky Dee.

She called Dale, her voice pitched just right, hopeful, defeated, desperate.

"Can we meet to discuss your offer of employment, please?"

Dale practically purred down the line. "Knew you'd see sense. I'll be over in an hour; need to see what I'm investing in. My clients are particular. Must be sure you fit the bill."

Exactly an hour later, Tissy opened her door and ushered the repulsive, overweight greaseball inside. Her performance was perfect: timid, shaky, compliant. She went into the kitchen to pour him a drink. But it wasn't her hand that delivered the glass. It was his... Micky Dee.

Dale recoiled, eyes bulging.

"Who the fuck are you? Do you know who I am?"

Micky's voice was calm, almost gentle, made it worse somehow. The menace was clear.

"Pay close attention to every word I say, Mister Paul Dale. I'm Micky Dee. That's M-I-C-K-Y D-E-E. I'm a friendly bloke. I like people. The only people I don't like are the kind who threaten women. Especially women who are my friends." He leaned in slightly, just enough for Dale to smell the truth behind the words.

"Tissy doesn't need your protection. She has mine. So, if you ever feel tempted to hassle her again... well, I find spontaneous violence works wonders. Messy, but effective. Do you understand me?" Dale swallowed hard.

"I—I'm sorry...didn't realise she was spoken for."

"Oh, she is," Micky said softly, "So let's have no more of this nonsense. I'll bid you a fond farewell."

Dale bolted for the door, tripping over the mat on his way out. When the lock clicked shut, Tissy drifted back into the room, a wicked smile tugging at her lips. She wrapped her arms around Mick's neck and whispered:

"I think I owe you one. Not in a hurry, are you?"

～

PAUL DALE KNEW that Micky Dee wasn't a man to be messed with. He hoped that he would never hear his name again - but he would.

Sooner than he had expected.

16

REPRISE

The voice broke into his thoughts like a match strike. He'd been content in the corner of the snug at 'The Brikkies', staring at a glass of Brandy he'd barely touched in twenty minutes. His usual haunt. His usual hour.

"Cheer up, bab—might never happen."

"I'm all right, Trina," he said, voice low, steady. "Just thinkin', reminiscing, that's all."

He found himself wondering, more often than he liked, where the last twenty-odd years had bled away to. Nearly a quarter of a century since they'd stamped him unfit, boxed up the only job he'd ever truly lived for, and shunted him out into the long shadows.

Every so often he'd cross paths with someone from the old days. Some would suddenly find the sky fascinating or bury their noses in phones they didn't need to check, anything to avoid the ghost walking towards them. Others would clasp his hand like a long-lost brother, genuinely pleased he was still breathing the same air. A few had never stopped returning his calls, their quiet favours over the years worth more than gold. But the ones who did speak to him, all of them, used the same line, said in a way that tried to be light but carried a weight he never quite knew how to hold.

'The legend, Mick Dorrington'. As if the title had replaced his first name. As if the myth mattered more than the man still dragging himself through the world. Of course, he recognised that 'legend' wasn't exclusively a complimentary term, but perhaps 'notorious' might have been more suited.

"Do you ever think about that night you came to my rescue... my knight in shining armour?" Trina gave a fake sigh.

He almost laughed. Knight? The man she meant had long since fallen off his horse. But he let her speak.

"It was twenty-something years ago," she said, "But feels like yesterday. I sometimes wonder where I'd be if you hadn't been in that pub. Gives me a shiver. I'd be a prisoner somewhere, owned by some creep and his filthy mates. Instead... well, I'm still a whore, but at least I'm a free one. And without you, I'd never have met Jacob and Harriett. I'd have had no one. You saved me. What brought you to me that night?" He shrugged, eyes somewhere else.

"Luck. Fate. Destiny. Maybe just your eyes and that shock of red hair. For a second I thought I knew you." She smiled, but it twitched, the way a smile does when it's trying to hide, "Well, whatever it was, I'll never thank you enough."

Mick frowned. He'd spent a life reading liars, lovers, killers and cowards. He could read Trina too.

"I think there's something you're not telling me," he murmured.

She gave a soft laugh, too soft, and shook her head. "There are no flies on you, Mick." Then she leaned forward, voice lowering into something troubled.

"There's someone I know... and I think she's walking straight into danger. I don't think she even realizes she needs help, but she does. I think she needs our help."

Mick didn't interrupt. He let her unwind the thread.

Trina told him about a teenage girl, fourteen, maybe fifteen, she'd seen hanging around Cannon Hill Park. Pretty kid, tidy, clean uniform, still going to school like nothing was wrong. But her parents were useless drunks, and she'd basically been raising herself. Trina had recognised her from their street. A neighbour. A forgotten child in a forgotten corner of Birmingham. And recently, too recently, the girl hadn't been alone.

"She was holding hands with a bloke," Trina said, "Much older. Early twenties, easy. She looked at him like he'd hung the moon for her." Mick felt a warning bell ring in his ribs.

Trina had engineered a little 'accidental' bump-into-on-the-way-home. Just girl talk. Just checking. The girl, Sky, had spilled the story in a breathless teenage gush.

"She met him in the park," Trina continued, twisting her fingers together. "Aiden, he calls himself. Said he was lonely. Bought her an ice cream. Told her he was from Manchester, just working down here for a bit. Then, after two weeks, told her he was in love with her but had to leave Birmingham soon."

She shook her head, eyes clouding, "Cruel trick, that. Especially for a kid who's never been loved properly."

Mick felt something shift inside him, a cold, familiar mechanism clicking neatly back into place. The old instincts sliding over him like a worn leather jacket he'd once sworn he'd never wear again.

"And now she's going to run away with him," Trina said, voice cracking, "She reckons they're going to spend the rest of their lives together."

Mick didn't speak. He let her continue.

"So I asked around," she said, "Wanted to know if any of the girls had seen anything dodgy. Annie, d'you know her? Nineteen but looks about fifteen, always in that schoolgirl outfit, caters for punters who like them on the young side, she told me she'd had a right laugh. Said some bloke approached her in the park, trying to chat her up like she was an actual schoolgirl. She told him to 'fuck off or she'd rip his bollocks off.'" Trina gave a humourless smile, "She didn't take much notice of him, but said he was about twenty, white guy, definitely a Scouser. Smart, decentlooking. Bit of a talker. That was by the park too."

Mick leaned forward, elbows on his knees. "Interesting. So, what does this Aiden look like? Same bloke?" Trina thought about it.

"Don't think so. Annie's sounded different. This Aiden... early twenties, tall, about your height. Broad across the shoulders. Light brown hair, dirty-blonde almost. Dark skin, West Indian in him, I'd bet. And his eyes..." She shivered, "Dark brown. Proper intense. He's a handsome lad. I can see why she's smitten. But Mick, he's lying to her. Leading her up the garden path. And she's just a child."

Mick nodded slowly. Calmly.

"Right. Something's going on here. And I've got a rough idea what it might be. So, how do I find him?"

"She's meeting him outside the café in the park. Midday. Saturday. That's when they're planning to do the big getaway." She met his eyes then , pleading, trusting, desperate, "We can stop this... can't we?"

Mick didn't answer straight away. He didn't need to. The look in his eyes did the talking.

"I'll need to make a couple of calls," he said at last, "Might need some support. I'll pick you up about ten on Saturday morning. Wear something smart. And flats, you'll thank me later."

And sitting there, in that worn old chair, Mick realised something he hadn't felt in years: that cold, terrible clarity. He was exactly the kind of man people called when the world was about to go wrong.

At precisely ten, Mick pulled up outside Trina's flat. She stepped out wearing a smart trouser suit and flats, red hair glowing, green eyes sharp. She looked stunning.

'She'll do nicely', he thought. He wore dark chinos, a navy polo shirt, black leather jacket, shoes polished to a shine. Nothing flashy. Just the kind of clean, composed look that made people behave.

They parked opposite Edgbaston Cricket Ground and walked together into the park café, bought coffees, and settled at one of the outside tables before eleven.

Half an hour later, Trina nudged him.

"That's him. He's early. What do we do?"

"Nothing yet. Follow my lead. Plenty of people around—he won't clock us. If he recognises you, just nod, keep talking."

Aiden drifted into view, bought two glasses of cola, and took a seat close enough that Mick could watch him without turning his head. The boy kept scanning the pathways...waiting.

Right on midday, Trina gave a small nod. Sky appeared reflected in the café's big window, dressed up as though for a date with a pop star, makeup thick, a small case in hand. Mick clocked two lads nearby watching her too. Spotters, by the look of them.

Sky ran the last few steps and threw her arms around Aiden's neck, smothering him with a kiss. He recoiled, barely a flicker, but unmistakable. A man who didn't like being touched by a child. He passed her the cola. She sipped, giggling. He checked his watch. Again, and again.

Mick made the decision.

He rose, moved like a man ambling nowhere in particular, and pulled up a chair beside Aiden. Trina mirrored him, taking the empty seat beside Sky.

Sky brightened.

"Trina! What are you doing here? Oh, this is Aiden, the love of my life."

Aiden froze. He started to stand, but Mick laid a firm hand on his shoulder.

"No. Sit down, son. We need a word and I think you know what about."

Aiden's face drained.

"I dunno what you're on about, mate. I'm just here with me girl. Right, Sky?" The Liverpool accent was obvious.

Sky blinked, confused. "What's going on, Trina? Who's this man?"

Mick's tone hardened. "Are you going to tell her, or shall I?" Panic set in. Real panic.

"You don't understand," Aiden whispered. "You don't know who you're messing with. They're watching. Right now. I'm fucked. You've got to help me."

"Oh aye?" Mick said quietly, "What do you suggest?"

Aiden swallowed, heavily. "You two look like Bizzies. Arrest me. Please. Take me away from here."

Sky burst into tears. "Aiden? What's happening? You love me, don't you?"

Mick stood and flashed a Tesco Clubcard like a warrant card.

"Aiden Green, you're under arrest," he said calmly, then cuffed him with a pair he'd kept from the job. The boy sagged with relief.

Two men in suits, Mick's "backup", rose from nearby tables, ready to escort them. A woman joined Sky, introducing herself in a soft, steady voice.

"Hello Sky. I'm Caroline Carey, Social Services. You're not in any trouble. You've been the victim of a cruel trick, and we're here to get you home safe."

Sky sobbed harder, but she let the woman guide her away.

And just like that, the pieces settled. The girl safe. The predator contained. The spotters already scattering, no stomach for a scene.

Mick walked Aiden toward the car, his hand firm on the lad's. shoulder. He could already tell this one wasn't going to kick off. There was no fight coiled in him, no bravado, none of that scally swagger Mick knew so well from the real predators he'd crossed swords with.

This boy looked almost relieved the whole sorry plan had been blown apart. Relieved that Sky was safe. Whatever else Aiden was, he wasn't a hardened Scouse villain. Mick had seen enough of them to recognise the breed. The panic the lad had shown earlier... Mick wasn't convinced it had been self-preservation. It felt more like genuine fear, of someone else. Of whatever pressure he'd been working under.

Maybe he'd been pushed into this. Maybe he hated himself for it. Mick couldn't be sure yet. But he knew one thing; when the moment came, Aiden would talk. He'd spill the whole story once he was somewhere safe, somewhere away from prying eyes.

The job wasn't finished. Not by a long stretch. But the sharpest edge of danger had passed. For now.

⁓

MICK HAD TOLD Trina she could head home, but she refused.

"I'm staying," she'd said, "Sky's going to have questions. Someone she knows should be there to answer them."

Aiden had heard every word from the back seat of Mick's car.

"Please... just tell her I'm sorry," he said, voice cracking under the weight of it, "She's a lovely girl. I never meant to hurt her. But I didn't have a choice. If it had just been me, I'd have told them to piss off. But it wasn't just me they had a grip on...I don't expect she'll forgive me. Probably better if she doesn't. She deserves someone good, someone her own age. Someone decent."

He sounded genuine—painfully so. Mick had met enough liars, predators and chancers to know the difference. There was a good lad buried in there somewhere...a good lad who'd taken a wrong turn and found the sort of men who never let their debts go unpaid. A pretty boy with charm enough to be useful—maybe too useful. The type who could con lonely women out of their savings if he had the stomach for it. But he didn't. Not really. His nerves gave him away. His fear felt like shame, not selfpreservation. No, this wasn't a budding monster. This was a guy being used.

He drove them into the city centre, parked in Livery Street as always, and walked the short distance to his office, an old Victorian place just off New Market Street. Nothing fancy, just enough polish to look respectable to new clients, and discreet enough to hide men who needed to talk.

Aiden was skittish, eyes darting at every sound.

Mick reassured him as they climbed the stairs, "No one followed us," he said, "You're safe here."

When they were all settled, Mick leaned forward, elbows on his knees.

"Start with your name. Full details."

"Aiden James Williams," the lad said quietly, "Born second of January, 2003 to a single mum. Never knew my dad."

Mick frowned, studying him more closely, as if something about the boy tugged at a locked drawer in his memory. But Aiden shook his head when asked the next question, confirming he'd never left

Liverpool until last year. He'd hadn't been born in Liverpool, but it had been his home since he was a toddler.

"Well," Mick said, "Where were you born then, if not Liverpool?"

Aiden flushed with embarrassment, "A little village called Flockton, near Wakefield."

Mick felt the hairs shift at the back of his neck, "Go on." Aiden swallowed hard.

"I've never told anyone this before. I was born in the Mother and Baby Unit at New Hall Prison. I was literally born doing time."

Mick's voice softened, "That must've been rough. What happened?"

Trina shot Mick a puzzled glance, none of this, as far as she could see, had anything to do with grooming teenage girls in Birmingham. But she kept quiet.

"My mum told me the story loads of times," Aiden continued, "She was involved with a drugs crew in Liverpool. Got five years. Served two-and-a-half. Left prison with more than she went in with... her words." He tried a small smile, "I was two and a bit when she got out." "And your father?", Mick asked.

Aiden shifted again, "I know she loved him. Said it wasn't a one-night thing. They lived together...proper relationship. She said he loved her too. Never loved anyone else after him."

"So what happened to him?"

"This is the bit that's confusing," Aiden said, "She was arrested in Liverpool, he wasn't. Either he'd been taken somewhere else or he'd got away. She wasn't sure. She only realised she was pregnant when she was on remand. It was a total shock. Whoever he was, my dad, he never knew. Even after she got out, she didn't try to find him. Said she worried it'd put him in danger."

A small shrug before he continued, "She always said I look a bit like him, same build, same face, same hair. Not the colour though. That's from her."

Before Mick could respond, Trina cut in sharply. "Hang on, you said she was shocked?"

"Yeah, completely shocked", Aiden responded.

"Why? If she'd been living with the bloke, your dad, why was she shocked to be pregnant?"

Aiden blinked, "She'd always believed she couldn't have kids."

Trina opened her mouth to ask something else, but Mick raised a hand like a traffic officer halting a lorry. He held it there for a long, silent fifty seconds, eyes narrowing as pieces fell into place, pieces he'd buried decades ago. Finally he spoke, voice barely above a whisper.

"So... your surname is Williams. And your mother's surname is Williams as well?"

"Yes, Michelle Williams" Aiden nodded. "She went back to her maiden name after I was born. Thought 'Aiden O'Grady' sounded too Irish."

Mick inhaled sharply, a long, full breath that didn't settle anywhere useful. Then he stood up so fast his chair shuddered back against the wall. He strode to the office door, opened it and said to Trina, "Stay with him for a moment."

Aiden blinked, "He must be desperate for the loo or something."

But Trina didn't believe that for a heartbeat. She knew, instinctively, that whatever had just clicked inside Mick Dorrington had nothing to do with toilets. And everything to do with ghosts.

MICK SAT IN HIS CAR, engine off, hands resting uselessly on the wheel, as the truth he'd just heard settled over him like falling ash. He'd joked for years about luck, fate, whatever phantom force seemed to steer him through tight corners and impossible situations. Privately he'd thanked it, wryly, almost superstitiously. But now that same invisible hand had dealt him a card so outrageous, so cruelly improbable, that even he struggled to believe it...Michelle.

He'd wondered about her now and then, in the quiet hours. Wondered where life had taken her, whether she'd found peace, happiness, anything softer than the world they'd both lived in. He'd wished her well, genuinely. But never, not once, had it crossed his mind that she might have had his child. It had been impossible. She couldn't have children. They had both believed that.

No wonder she'd been shocked to learn she was pregnant. No wonder everything had unraveled so strangely in those final days before the arrests. She must have discovered it while still on remand, alone, terrified, and unable to tell him.

And one man had known all along. Detective Superintendent David "Jock" McAllister. Officer in Charge and Architect of the operation. The man who'd coerced Michelle into helping take down Victor Harland, who had groomed Mick and manipulated every move he made, who had quietly removed every truth that didn't suit his agenda. McAllister had known she was pregnant. He had known she was carrying Mick's child.

"Do not try and contact her."

Those words echoed now with a different weight entirely. Was that meant to protect Michelle? To protect Mick? Or had McAllister simply feared that if Mick discovered the truth, if he knew she was pregnant, knew she needed him, the whole case would come crashing down around them? The case McAllister had been obsessed with. The case he'd sacrificed Mick for. The case he'd sacrificed Michelle for. Mick closed his eyes.

The betrayal ran deeper than even he had imagined. In that moment, just fleetingly, he wanted to hurt McAllister. He wanted everyone to know the sort of man he was.

Colleagues, family, friends, neighbours, everyone. They all needed to know exactly what he was. For now though, Mick had a job to do. He had to play a role. He had to play the role of Aiden's interrogator, not his long-lost, long-forgotten father.

MICK STRODE BACK into the office with purpose.

Trina glanced up, concern creasing her brow.

"Are you all right, bab?"

He nodded once—sharp, certain.

"I'm fine. But I'm going to want to hear exactly how you", he looked straight at Aiden, "got yourself mixed up in this business. Every detail. Dot every 'i', cross every 't', and don't try selling me any bullshit, I can smell it a mile off. Over to you, Aiden. In your own words, let's hear it."

Truth was, Mick already had the shape of the story in his head. He could have recited most of it himself. But he needed to hear it from the lad's own mouth.

Aiden drew a breath, "I grew up in Liverpool thinking life was all right. I'd forgotten where I was born, forgotten Mum being in prison, by the time I started school. She gave me everything I needed, and loads I didn't. I reckon she wanted to make sure I never felt the gap where my dad should've been." He shifted in his seat, gathering himself.

"My aunt Sarah and my uncle Jamie... they were always around. Proper close. Great Christmases, birthdays, all that. Aunt Sarah used to say, 'You're the image of your father, lad, same face, same build, but you've got your mum's eyes and colouring'. Sometimes mom would look at me like it hurt her, like I reminded her of him."

He paused and swallowed hard before continuing, "It was about 2016, maybe 2017, I'd have been fourteen, fifteen, when Mum, Aunt Sarah and Uncle Jamie sat down to talk about something big. I didn't know what it was, but they were terrified. For two years they lived on edge. Checking under the car for bombs. Jumping every time someone knocked at the door. They were expecting trouble. Then... nothing."

Mick spoke quietly, though he already knew the answer, "So, did you ever find out what they were afraid of?"

Aiden nodded, a thin smile flickering.

"Yeah. Eventually. It's the reason I'm here now. There was a Liverpool gangster banged up around the same time as Mom. She'd worked for him, his accountant. Dunno if he blamed her for everything, but he never trusted her again. Aunt Sarah and Uncle Jamie were scared he'd want revenge." Again he paused, "Didn't matter in the end. Other crews took over while he was inside. He left the country, got out while he could. No contact with Mum. Nothing with anyone in Liverpool, as far as I know."

He drew a shaky breath, "Then last year he turns up again, back in Liverpool, and starts looking up old contacts. Uncle Jamie first. Then Mum. She told me later he'd given up on the drugs game. Found something more profitable and less risky, people smuggling. Young girls groomed for the sex trade."

Trina's breath caught, but Aiden pressed on.

"He was too well known in Liverpool, didn't have the clout he used to, so he started working south, Manchester, Stoke, Wolves, Birmingham. Getting local lads to do the chatting-up. Scouse humour, charm, confidence. Perfect for it. They'd find teenage girls, get 'em up to Liverpool, get 'em on smack or Charlie till they were hooked... then use 'em. Here or overseas," he rubbed both hands over his face and carried on, "Then he saw me and that was that. Told me I worked for him now. I said I didn't want to. Didn't matter. He made it clear, if I didn't bring him girls, proper young ones, then Mum could have a nasty accident - a fatal one." His voice broke,

"That's why I got involved. Didn't want to. I didn't have a choice. It was either do what he wanted... or wait for him to hurt mum. I told her that I was going to the police. I thought we could go into protection or something, but she said that he still knew too many people who would point him in our direction. We would never be safe. Finally. I thought I had no option...but I think there is one option left to me. I think I am going to have to end it. End him, for good".

Mick responded immediately, "If you do that, you will ruin your life, your mom's life, and the lives of those you love and who love you. I'm quite a big believer in Karma. Those who live by the sword shall die by the sword. Now then, there is just one detail that you haven't told me; this gangsters name."

Aiden hesitated, "Karma?"

Mick sensed his reluctance. "Okay, let me give you a name, shall I? Victor Harland".

Aiden almost choked. "Are you one of his..?"

Mick reassured him. "No, he is someone I once knew, but I'm not one of his people if that was what you were going to ask. I do understand the type of man you're dealing with though. I'm going to give you a story about what happened to you today, after you were 'arrested'. It is important that you are comfortable telling Harland the story. He must not suspect anything, are we clear?"

Aiden was perfectly clear and Mick ran through the procedure that he would have gone through if he had been arrested. Where he was taken. What he was asked. How he replied. Basically he thought Sky was at least sixteen, she certainly looked older with her makeup on, and she'd told him that she was over sixteen. Luckily, Sky didn't complain, she confirmed what Aiden had said and he was eventually released without charge. That was the story advised.

When Mick was certain that Aiden had understood what he was to say, he had one final instruction for him. But first asked Trina if she would mind stepping outside for a few minutes.

Mick then thought for a minute or two, clearly weighing up Aiden's chances of being able to deliver what he was about to suggest.

"Right," he said at last, leaning back, "You want out. I want Harland's reach cut off from your mum, from her family, from anyone he thinks he owns. We're not going to manage all that in one afternoon, but we can start."

Aiden swallowed. "He's not going to just let me walk away."

"He may not allow you to walk away," Mick replied, "He just needs to believe you're still useful. And that, for now, it is far better if you keep your head down and put some distance between you and him." "A lie," Aiden said.

"A tailored version of the truth," Mick corrected him, "You did meet Sky. You did plan to run. We stopped you, and your spotters saw you getting arrested. But when he asks what happened next—and he will —you tell him this..."

He laid it out carefully, watching the lad's face, checking each beat landed where it needed to.

"You say that, when you were in the station, they asked if you wanted a solicitor. You said yes, but you didn't know anyone. They got you a local brief from their call-out list. This is his card."

He slid one of Dawkins' business cards across the desk.

"Then tell Harland you were put in a holding cell until your brief arrived. While you were in the cells, you overheard a couple of detectives talking in the corridor. One of them mentioned a name—said something like, 'Mikey Vaughan... back in the UK. Dutch were supposed to have buried him."

Aiden's brow tightened, "I've heard that name before".

Mick continued, "Tell him you heard them say Vaughan's sent some boys up to Liverpool looking for the bloke he blames for the Dutch arrest. And one of them laughed, 'Some Scouse gangster's going to get slotted,' that's the line. You all right with that?"

"You think he'll believe it?" Aiden asked.

"With a bit of window dressing, yes," Mick replied, "Leave the window dressing to me."

Aiden bit his lip. "What do I say about the arrest? How did I get out of it?"

"Easy," Mick explained, "When your solicitor arrived, he asked why you'd been nicked. The cops said they'd had a tip-off about an older lad sniffing around schoolgirls in Cannon Hill Park. They spotted you with a young girl. But she told them she'd told you that she was over sixteen. You'd kissed her, nothing more." He shrugged, "So the brief says, 'No complaint, no offence. Why's my client still locked up?' After he left, they ran your name, gave you a warning, told you to stay out of Birmingham. And that they'd circulate your photo nationwide, part of some new county-lines sex trafficking initiative."

Aiden frowned. "So, he'll swallow that?"

"He wants to swallow it," Mick said, "You're more useful to him uncharged. That's how he thinks. He'll give you time for the heat to die down, keep you on the shelf for later."

Aiden hesitated. "And Vaughan? Like I say, I've heard that name before."

"So has Harland," Mick replied, "It'll give him something else to worry about—someone else."

"You want him looking at Vaughan instead of my mum," Aiden murmured.

"Yes," Mick said. "You won't mention your mum. You won't mention Jamie. You won't mention anything you've told me in this room.

You give him the story and keep your mouth shut."

"And if he doesn't buy it?"

Mick held his gaze, steady and cold, "Then you've got bigger problems than I can fix in one chat. But he will. Men like Harland always do the sums. They always take the easiest path."

Aiden nodded slowly. "So I go back. Tell him I got nicked. Tell him they let me go. Tell him some Brummie's out for revenge."

"Not just some Brummie," Mick said softly, "Mikey Vaughan, and make sure you say the coppers were laughing, that they wouldn't want to be the Scouser who'd crossed him."

He leaned closer, "You get back to Liverpool. No detours. When he's done with you, you ring me from a phone that can't be traced. After that, you're finished with him. Whatever he asks, whatever he threatens, you're done. Understood?"

"And my mum?" Aiden said quietly.

"We'll get to your mum," Mick told him, "One thing at a time."

17

KARMA

Harland's office sat at the back of a converted warehouse on the Mersey, bare brick, smoked glass, leather furniture that looked untouched by human hands. Aiden perched on the edge of a chair that probably cost more than his mum's car.

The man sitting at the desk poured himself a whisky. He didn't offer one to Aiden. He never offered drinks to the kids. Kept hierarchy clear.

"So," Harland said, turning slow, "Birmingham." His voice was calm, but the room tightened around it.

Tom O'Dowd leaned by the door, arms folded. Another lad loitered by the window.

Aiden swallowed, "Yeah, Birmingham."

"You were meant to bring me a girl," Harland said, "And instead, I get a call saying you've vanished and some woman, social worker maybe, has taken her home in tears. That's not what we agreed."

"No", Aiden murmured. "It went sideways".

"Tell me exactly what happened.

Aiden told the story exactly as Mick had drilled into him: the café, Sky running into his arms, the arrest, the questioning, the solicitor.

"And they let you go?" Harland said, unimpressed.

"Yeah, Sky told them I thought she was over sixteen. Said nothing had happened. They believed her. And…"

"And…?" Harland pushed. "Something your not telling me lad. Spit
it out"

Aiden inhaled.

"When they put me in the cells, I heard two coppers talking. They mentioned someone. A name you know."

Harland's eyes hardened. "A name I know?"

"Mikey Vaughan. I've heard you mention him." O'Dowd straightened.

Aiden continued quickly, "They said he was back. Said the Dutch had let him go. Said he thought a Scouse gangster set him up years ago and that he's sent blokes up here looking for whoever it was." Harland stared at him for a long, silent stretch.

"You tell them anything about me?"

"No, I never mentioned your name. Course not," Aiden said instantly, "Nothing. I said I met her online. They checked me out, saw I had no record, gave me a warning, told me my details would be circulated to other regions, or something, mentioned county border something, and then they kicked me out."

More silence.

Then Harland turned away, staring out at the grey river beyond the smoked glass.

"You're done". he then said.

Aiden blinked, "What? I can still help."

"No more Birmingham or anywhere else for now. No more girls. No more anything. You're someone they'll keep an eye out for. Get a job for a while. You look after your mum. You keep your head down. If anyone asks about me, you don't know a thing," he paused, "If I find out you've lied, then you understand that I'll take it out on someone you care about," Harland threatened, his eyes showing he meant every word.

Tom O'Dowd opened the door. "Off you go, lad."

Aiden stepped out. The door closed. Through the wood he caught the tail of a conversation:

"You think the kid's right, Vic? About Vaughan?"

Harland's reply was low. "Doesn't matter what he thinks. What matters is what I know, and if that bastard's still breathing, he'll be looking for me. I'm not scared of him, but right now I'm not in a position to face off with him. My day will come. But for now, Mikey Vaughan is an inconvenience that I don't need"."

～

THAT EVENING and the next day, Harland received several calls from contacts. Same story, different mouths.

"Couple of strangers knocking round the docks, flashing your photo, asking where you drink... offering money."

"Brummies. Bikers in leather. Lads in trench coats. Definitely not cops".

The 'window dressing'. A handful of Mick's old undercover mates, professionals at radiating danger. By the time the whispers reached Harland, they'd been twisted into something worse. 'Mikey Vaughan is coming'.

Harland wasn't scared, he never had been, but this was a fight he couldn't win. Not here. Not now. He began making arrangements.

～

"YOU DID WELL," Mick said.

They sat in a lay-by off the East Lancs Road. Aiden still looked shell-shocked.

"He's let me go. Just like that."

"For now," Mick replied, "Men who feel hunted don't like amateurs under their feet."

Aiden nodded, "At least he believed the Vaughan story."

"Of course he did."

Aiden hesitated. "Do you think he'll try to get to Vaughan first?"

"If he does," Mick said, "that'll be his mistake."

~

A COUPLE OF DAYS LATER, Mick dropped in on Dawkins, his lawyer friend.

"Well, old boy?" Dawkins grinned, "Judging from your face, everything went swimmingly."

"So far," Mick said, "If anyone rings you asking if you've done any duty-solicitor work recently, mention representing a lad from Liverpool who got nicked chatting up a fourteen-year-old. Add your usual theatrical garnish. They'll lap it up."

"My pleasure. And I may have another morsel of work for you..."

Mick shook his head, "I'm taking two weeks in Scarborough. Caravan site. Middle of nowhere. Phone off. Might have a friend visiting."

"You naughty boy," Dawkins teased.

~

TWO WEEKS LATER, Dawkins called in on Mick at his canal side flat. Not necessarily unusual, but this time he looked even more animated than usual.

"Come on through to the kitchen. Just made a pot of tea. Real tea, none of this tea bag nonsense."

Dawkins seemed pleased to see his good friend.

"If you've come for a stick of Scarborough rock, afraid I didn't bring any back this time."

Dawkins dropped a newspaper on Mick's kitchen table so hard the pot of tea rattled.

"Page three, old boy," he said. "You might want to have a look." Mick didn't hurry. He finished his mouthful, wiped his hands on a tea towel, and only then reached for the paper.

The headline was blunt.

'BRITISH GANGSTER SHOT DEAD OUTSIDE MARBELLA VILLA'

The grainy photograph underneath was unmistakable.

'Sources say the deceased, Victor Harland, 54, had been drinking with associates at a popular bar in the Costa del Sol resort. After leaving, he had walked a short distance to his villa, and as he stood on his doorstep he had been fatally wounded by a single bullet to the back of his head'.

Mick kept reading. There was mention of a suspected 'settling of old scores', of 'links to historic drug trafficking in the North West', of 'a man once described in court as untouchable'. No arrests. Police are appealing for witnesses who may have witnessed the shooting, or who saw a motorcycle that had been heard roaring off from the area just after shots had been heard.

Dawkins watched him closely, "Ring any bells?"

"Of course," Mick said immediately, "That operation I did in Liverpool. He was the target. Bloody hell old boy, can't believe someone's seen him off. Course, he'd upset a lot of the old faces by taking over their businesses. Only a matter of time, I suppose."

"Forgive me, Dorrington, but whenever British gangsters start getting ventilated abroad, I always wonder where you've been holidaying."

"You know where I was going. A couple of quiet weeks in 'Scarbados', on the North Yorkshire Riviera."

"Uh-huh," Dawkins didn't sound convinced, "Any idea who might have wanted Harland ventilated?"

"How long have you got?" Mick replied, "He had a queue."

Dawkins studied him for a long moment before continuing the conversation.

"You know, it's the most damming thing," he said at last, "Your name still comes up in old files. Harland this, Vaughan that. Every time I read one, I think, 'if anyone ever writes all this down, no bugger will believe a word of it'."

Mick folded the paper carefully, "Good, let's keep it that way."

Eventually Dawkins picked up his briefcase. "Anyway, thought you'd want to see it. I'll get out of your hair. I've got a judge to charm."

On the way out, the lawyer shouted back, "One hell of a good tan you got in Scarborough, old boy. Byeee."

When the door clicked shut, Mick read the article again, slowly, then put the paper away in a drawer. On the counter beside him, his mobile buzzed. A new message, from an unregistered number.

'Heard about VH. Mom says she can sleep again. Karma?– A.'

Mick stared at the screen for a long time before deleting the text.

An hour or so later, another message from another unregistered number.

'Bro, all good. Any time. T - wow!'

Mick smiled and said quietly to himself, "Cheers Bro, glad you had fun!"

At 2pm that same day, Mick received a call from a Scarborough number.

"Mr. Michael Dorrington? It's the Scarborough Sun Salon, here. Our cleaner has just found a gold neck chain with the initials 'MD' on it. Looking at our records, I think you were the only customer at the salon in the last week or so who has those initials. Is it yours?"

"It is! I've been looking all over for it. I'll be back up in a few weeks' time and I'll call in then, if you can keep it safe for me please."

Mick put the phone down and whispered to himself, "Window dressing. Cheers bro!"

18

CALL ME JOCK

The takedown of Victor Harland's empire was the kind of case that forged legends, and no one burnished his own glory harder than Jock McAllister. While Mick worked in the dark, bruised and breaking, Jock basked in the fluorescent light of briefing rooms and ministerial praise.

By 2006 the had been awarded the Queens Police Medal (QPM), official recognition for "exceptionally meritorious conduct." The citation applauded his calm command during a difficult covert operation and even commended the way he'd "supported and managed" an undercover officer whose judgement had allegedly begun to unravel.

Those words, supported, managed, looked noble in the citation. They hid the pressure, the manipulation, the broken promises, the deception. Jock always knew how to dress his ambition in the language of duty.

On paper, he looked untouchable. A Superintendent with medals, connections, and a reputation chiselled from stone. But after the QPM ceremony, something curious happened.

Nothing.

No promotion. No fresh posting. No gentle nudge toward command. The ladder simply stopped beneath his feet. Most officers would have accepted that, Superintendent was a rank most never reached. But those who knew Jock, or thought they did, found his stagnation perplexing. And Jock himself felt the slight like a blade slipped between the ribs. He had played the game, done what needed doing, shaped and steered events towards outcomes he thought would carry him further. He believed he had earned the ascent.

Among the rank and file, people muttered. Among the brass, they whispered. The two doctors who had evaluated Mick, those prophets of professional doom, had apparently raised concerns about Jock as well. Nothing written, nothing official, but words passed in careful tones: questions about judgement, emotional instability, decisions made for reasons other than operational need. No accusations, just the kind of quiet doubts that kill careers without ever appearing in a single document.

Enough, though, for someone very senior to take him aside and suggest, kindly but firmly, that he consider viewing the QPM as a career full stop rather than a comma.

In 2008, Jock retired.

He bought a small cottage on the outskirts of Edinburgh, quiet, beautiful, the sort of place he once imagined would represent peace. But peace is not something that arrives just because a man stops working. For Jock, it never arrived at all. Friends who visited him in the early years described a man slowly turning inward, stewing over decisions no longer relevant, reliving slights real and imagined. The bitterness did not flare; it seeped, like damp seeps through brick.

His marriage floundered under the weight of his unhappiness. His bitterness, like a virus, spread and affected everyone around him.

His wife left in 2012; the divorce followed in due course. After that, he withdrew further. Calls went unanswered, visits dwindled. He became the kind of quiet absence people notice only in hindsight.

Three years later, Jock died alone, his heart, worn down by years of resentment, giving out in the small hours. It was nearly a week before a neighbour, concerned by the stillness of the cottage, alerted the authorities.

Mick never learned what became of him. Their fates had diverged long before. And perhaps it was better that Mick never heard the details. Some endings, he had come to understand, belong not to justice or vengeance, but simply to time. Mick had't forgiven, but he had forgotten.

And when you are not paying attention, time, more than any enemy Mick had ever faced, had a talent for closing accounts quietly.

19

AND , FINALLY.

The café at Albert Dock had changed names three times since the days of Mikey Vaughan, but the view was the same: red brick, grey water, gulls circling tourists.

Mick took a corner table. Old habits.

Trina sat opposite. "You sure about this, bab?"

"No," Mick said, "But that's never stopped me before." The door chimed.

Michelle O'Grady, now Michelle Williams, stepped inside. Shorter hair, a few greys, same eyes. Aiden hovered behind her.

Trina waved them over.

Michelle's gaze lingered on Mick. "So you're him…"

"Mick Dorrington," he said quietly, "Or Mikey Vaughan, depends who's talking."

She let out a short, brittle laugh, "You don't do anything by halves."

They sat with Aiden looking as if he was waiting for a verdict.

"Before anything else," Mick said, "I'm sorry for Harland; for McAllister. For the whole bloody mess. If my ego hadn't got the better of me, I'd never have listened to Jock McAllister. None of this would have happened. Okay, you'd still be running the books for Harland, but. . . "

Michelle studied him, "And yet here we all are. That's something."

Trina cut in gently. "We're not here for blame. We're here for truth."

Mick nodded before turning to Aiden.

"You know most of it. The case. The lies. How they used all of us. But there's one bit no one told you. Because I didn't know." Michelle's hands shook. She clasped them hard.

"Your mom, Aiden," Mick said, "She thought she couldn't have kids. I thought she couldn't have kids. The doctors had told her so. When I found out she'd had a child... it was like the ground shifted."

Michelle whispered, "Tell him."

Mick looked at the lad properly this time, saw himself in the line of his jaw, the stubborn set of his mouth.

"Truth is, I'm your father, Aiden," he said, "For whatever that's worth."

The silence that followed was raw and fragile.

"You could be lying," Aiden said.

"I could," Mick agreed, "But I'm not."

Michelle added softly, "We can prove it. DNA, whatever you want."

Aiden swallowed. "Did you know? When Harland sent me to Birmingham?"

"No," Michelle said instantly, "I never knew it was him. Not until Trina rang. She gave me the whole story."

Then she looked at Mick, her eyes filling with tears, "I really loved you. I never stopped loving you. I wanted to be with you, but I was put in a position that made me hurt you...us. If you hated me, I would under......".

He sharply interrupted, "It took a while for me to put all the pieces together, but when I did, I knew that you had no choice. I have never hated you. Despite the years, despite everything that has happened, I still feel the same love for you as I did when I first looked into your gorgeous eyes.." Trina coughed.

Aiden joked, "Blimey you two, get a room," he then looked down, "Seriously, so what now?"

"Now?" Mick asked, "Whatever you want. You walk out; I won't chase you. You stay... we figure it out. Slow. Proper. As ourselves." Michelle reached out, one hand for her son, the other for Mick.

"One condition," she said.

"Anything. Name it," promised Mick.

"No more lies. If you're in his life, if you are my life, you do it as Mick. Not Mikey. Not Micky. Just you."

Mick nodded with a wry smile, "Deal."

Outside, the Liverpool sky was its usual grey, but on the horizon, a thin line of pale brightness was beginning to break through and for the first time in years, Mick Dorrington let himself imagine it might just possibly, be moving their way.

ABOUT THE AUTHOR

V. J. Harris

V. J. Harris is a former British police officer whose three decades of service included extensive work in undercover roles across the UK and overseas. Drawing on those years spent operating in the shadows —immersed in dangerous criminal networks, walking the blurred line between truth and deception—Harris brings an unparalleled authenticity to his debut novel. His insight into long-term infiltration work, and the psychological cost paid by those who undertake it, gives Shadow Line its gritty realism and emotional depth.

Printed in Dunstable, United Kingdom

78179651R00119